'Hi, Linc. Thanks for stopping by to collect me.'

She got the words out before she looked at him properly. It was just as well, because when she did she couldn't drag her gaze away again.

He had on a sleek evening suit in a dark, pin-striped grey, a crisp white shirt and a thin powder-blue tie. Polished black dress shoes completed the outfit, and as he moved his arm slightly she caught a glimpse of a gold cufflink.

Oh.

My.

Gosh.

Could any man look more handsome than Linc did tonight?

Dear Reader,

What a journey it has been for the MacKay brothers. First Brent found his wonderful partner, Fiona, and then Alex found the beautiful Jayne. Now it is finally Linc's turn to find love, and his plant nursery manager Cecilia Tomson is just the woman to help him along that path. Or perhaps I should say through that maze, for Linc will have to take an internal journey of discovery, acceptance and understanding before he is finally able to allow himself to reach out fully for love.

Much of Cecilia's romantic heart has gone into the creation of the Fleurmazing plant nursery, with its delightful flowering feature maze. Her work at the nursery has helped Cecilia through some tough times, and she has an even tougher road ahead before she will finally reach the fulfilment of her own personal love story…with Linc.

I hope you enjoy the journey with them as Linc and Cecilia follow their special pathway to love. I found great joy in writing about them.

From Australia, with all *my* love,

Jennie Adams

TEMPTED BY HER TYCOON BOSS

BY
JENNIE ADAMS

Published in Great Britain 2016
By Mills & Boon, an imprint of HarperCollins*Publishers*
1 London Bridge Street, London, SE1 9GF

© 2016 Jennie Adams

ISBN: 978-0-263-26403-6

Our policy is to use papers that are natural, renewable and recyclable
products and made from wood grown in sustainable forests. The logging
and manufacturing processes conform to the legal environmental
regulations of the country of origin.

Printed and bound in Great Britain
by CPI Antony Rowe, Chippenham, Wiltshire

After years of living in a small inland city in New South Wales, Australia, **Jennie Adams** re-embraced the country lifestyle of her childhood. When she isn't writing Jennie dedicates her time to promoting the natural wonders of her new area and encouraging others to visit and enjoy what now constitutes her back yard—large tracts of native bushland, flora and fauna reserves, and wetlands. Jennie's family has grown to embrace in-laws (and outlaws, as she always jokes), sisters, daughters and brothers of the heart. Find Jennie at joybyjennie.com.

Books by Jennie Adams

Mills & Boon Romance

Daycare Mum to Wife
Once Upon a Time in Tarrula
Invitation to the Prince's Palace

Visit the Author Profile page at millsandboon.co.uk for more titles.

For my dad. You were my first storyteller
and you'll always remain the best to me.
Love you.

CHAPTER ONE

'GOOD MORNING, CECILIA.' Linc MacKay spoke the greeting as he stepped between shoulder-height hedge shapes bursting from within with raised flowering displays. 'Your second-in-command told me I'd probably find you here.'

'Here' was the feature maze area of the Fleurmazing Plant Nursery on its acreage just outside the Sydney city limits. The Australian sun warmed the air, and the light breeze carried the scents of a summer garden.

Now it had also brought a handsome millionaire, stepping around a corner of the maze to an alcove where a statue of a sun goddess draped in gossamer folds reached her arms upwards as though to bless the world with her light.

Was it the soft look in Linc's eyes as his gaze moved beyond the sun goddess and lingered on her that made Cecilia's breath suddenly catch? A moment later the expression disappeared, if it had ever truly been there at all.

'Linc. Is it that time already?' She focused on projecting professionalism into her words and tried to push those discomforting questions to the back of her mind. 'I'm glad Jemmie was able to point you in the right direction to find me.'

Cecilia placed one final hedge trimming into the basket over her arm and walked towards the plant nursery's owner. If she didn't feel entirely calm she could at least act as though she were.

'This is my favourite part of the maze, to be honest.'

'I can see why.' His gaze took in the maze, its beautiful flowers every shade from creamy white to deepest violet and blue. But then he turned back and took in Cecilia, too, from the top of her honey-blond hair in its high ponytail, over her face, lingering on each feature, and quickly sweeping over the simple strappy sundress that showed off her curves to perfection.

She rarely dressed in her best girly attire for work but, knowing that today she'd be inside most of the day in the office, Cecilia had let her most feminine side have its way.

'It's stunning,' Linc finally said. 'The…ah…the maze.'

'Thank you.' She drew a slightly unsteady breath. 'I'm sorry I wasn't up front, ready to greet you.'

Cecilia glanced at the trimmings in the basket over her arm and hoped by doing so she would disguise her swirling thoughts from him.

'This is a never-ending job.'

'And a very important one at the moment, I can imagine.'

Why, oh, *why* did she have to feel suddenly oh-so-conscious of him? She had much better control than this. Usually…

Wasn't it enough that she'd mistaken his interest once before, years ago?

'The maze needs to look good. Fantastic, in fact.'

She forced the words out and told herself to concentrate on matters at hand. The Fleurmazing plant nursery was the third and most recent of Linc's Sydney plant nurseries that she had managed over the six years she'd been in his employ, but this one was different.

It was *her* brainchild—a holistic nursery that required greater upkeep but offered an enhanced experience for its visitors. At least in this aspect of her life she had it together!

She should keep her focus on that. Now, of all times, Cecilia needed to 'sell' the nursery's virtues to Linc at any opportunity she got. Noticing his character traits or wondering if his attention was caught on her wasn't part of that plan.

'We're logging hundreds of people every day, who all come here specifically because they want to experience the maze. Sales out of that alone are fantastic. And the maze needs to be perfect in time for the part we're playing in Sydney's Silver Bells charity flower show, so I'm giving it a lot of attention at the moment.'

'A masked ball in the middle of a plant maze is ambitious.' One side of his mouth kicked up. 'But I'm sure if anyone can carry it off it'll be you.'

'The Silver Bells organisers have put their faith in me, so I have no choice now.' She said it laughingly, but the importance of it was never far from her thoughts.

She wouldn't have had the opportunity if Linc hadn't agreed to let her take the risk.

'It'll pay off, Linc. Your whole chain of plant nurseries will get good attention out of our participation in the Silver Bells event.'

Linc owned a dozen nurseries across the city, along with bucketloads of real estate and a commodities trading portfolio that, on its own, probably ran into millions. He truly was the quintessential millionaire bachelor, with the world at his feet. They were more than poles apart, which had made her *faux pas* of throwing herself at him six years ago even more embarrassing.

He hadn't been interested. She'd mistaken his charming way for something it wasn't, and then— moments after he'd let Cecilia down as gently as anyone possibly could have—a woman had arrived for her lunch date with him. A sophisticated older woman.

Old news, Cee. Linc played the gentleman that day, apologised that he'd given the wrong impression and went off on his date with Ms Socialite while you went back to digging around in potting mix. And you got over it.

Cecilia had worked hard to impress him professionally since then, and she'd dated. Then she'd found Hugh, and that relationship had lasted almost two years. Linc had no doubt dated lots more versions of Ms Socialite, too, though Cecilia had not heard of him ever being in a serious long-term relationship since she'd known him.

'I appreciate you coming in for the business review. I know you're busy. Actually, I thought you might have sent someone to do it for you.'

'You've earned this opportunity, and I felt I owed

it to you to undertake the review myself.' Sincerity rang in his tone. 'I want to grant you that twenty per cent share in the nursery if I can, and no one else will understand your work here and your vision the way that I do.'

That was true. Even though the bulk of their inter-actions were over the phone, she'd always reported regularly to Linc.

And she'd negotiated—refusing bonuses over the years in favour of building up to this: a chance to own a share in the nursery. One day she wanted to open her own business.

'I hope the review proves my efforts worthy of your time.'

Linc might have rejected her overtures, but he had been her example since he'd first taken her on and let her manage one of his nurseries six years ago, with no experience and only her determination to get her through. He was proof that a person could achieve anything if they wanted it enough.

What would he be now? Thirty-four? Thirty-five? Still with the same deep timbre to his voice, the same way of wearing his work boots, jeans and chambray shirt with an authority overlaid with a deceptive dose of casual charm.

With a strong chin, short-cut dark hair, those gor-geous shoulders and a way of carrying himself that shouted, *Look out, world!* Linc MacKay was in all ways a force to be reckoned with.

Linc would be making the nursery his base while he undertook the review. They'd be spending quite a bit of time in each other's company. It couldn't be a worse time for that old awareness of him to resurface. Whatever had brought it back, she needed her interest in him *gone*. Now, if not sooner.

Cecilia began the return walk towards the equipment shed and the front office.

'I know I'll see good results here, Cecilia. With each new nursery you've managed, you've improved on the last.' Linc fell into step beside her in the maze. 'I *have* taken it all in, you know—including the way this one has exceeded all expectations. Bringing coach tours in on a daily basis, gaining that whole new layer of tourism clientele…that has shown real vision.'

His words made every moment of her hard work feel doubly worth it. Cecilia couldn't help smiling as she quietly thanked him.

'Our social media presence has made a difference, too. I'm blessed to have Jemmie here, with her skills in photography and videography. Her plants-growing-and-bursting-into-flower videos get a lot of attention online.'

'You found a good asset in her.'

His compliment pleased her, but it was his simple gesture for her to precede him through a narrower section of the maze that brought back that earlier flutter to Cecilia's pulse. It felt *intimate* to her. As though they'd met here for a morning tryst and were returning now to their 'real' lives.

How silly.

Planning for this masked ball must be messing with her brain. Cecilia couldn't come up with a more feasible explanation for her sudden case of hyper-Linc-awareness.

Or perhaps you've simply been out of your rela-

*tionship with Hugh long enough to open your eyes
and look around you?*

If so, she could cast her attention in some other
direction, thank you very much. Because Linc was
not for her and she'd accepted that fact and got over
caring about it a very long time ago.

She *had*, right…?

'Thank you, Linc, for the commitment you've
made to do this review.'

If the words were a little stiff and formal, that
couldn't be helped. Surely that was better than falling all over him, even if only inside her own thoughts.

'I know it's time away from the other demands of
your life.'

'I suspect some of those demands will follow me
here, but I'll do my best not to disrupt you.' A teasing smile came and went.

Cecilia ignored how that smile made her tummy
flutter. It had to be the kind of smile that one friend
might share with another, or a person who'd known
another person for years, or a boss who felt comfortable with his employee. And Cecilia fell into the lat-
ter category. Yes, she'd known Linc for years, but
they were work associates with a lot of *professional*
ground walked over in that span of time.

Therefore his smile must be a perfectly normal one
that meant nothing whatsoever outside those bounds.
He couldn't help it if he was cute.

Great avoiding of his appeal, Cee.

He went on. 'I don't want to make a painful time
out of this for you.'

'I'm sure it will be fine.' No matter the outcome,
she knew Linc would be fair in his assessment.

Whether she could eliminate the painful knowledge of her reawakened awareness of him was another challenge altogether.

But it was one that she had to achieve, and she could not let the rest of her life mess with her head, either, while she got through the review. That would be easier said than done, when one part of it gnawed at her ceaselessly and she was still stinging over another part.

Well, no-longer-interested-and-nothing-could-keep-me-here-now Hugh could go and trip over and fall into a duck pond, for all she cared. And the other thing just...*was.*

Cecilia drew a breath.

Her personal life might not be as calm as she would like, but she could manage—and Linc didn't need to know about any of it.

She detoured to leave her plant cuttings and basket in the potting shed, and then led the way to her office. 'Come on in. How long do you think the review will take?'

'Depending on how much I get interrupted, it shouldn't take more than a few days.'

His gaze searched hers just a little bit too keenly for her comfort.

'Great.' She gestured to where a second computer and desk sat at a diagonal angle to her own, and pushed those other thoughts as far back in her mind as she could manage. 'I don't mean it's great that you won't be here more than that. You know what I mean...'

Did he? Was he hearing her words falling over themselves in a way that was quite out of character after her usual modulated approaches to him?

So get over it, Cecilia. You've been to see him at his city office, where the staff all complain that he's hardly ever there but say it fondly, as though they're glad that he gives them the autonomy to do their best for him while he's out spreading his holdings even further. You've been to the warehouse home he shared in the past with his brothers. He's seen you at each of the nurseries you've managed. Multiple times, in fact. This is no different.

'The financials are all on there.' She used her best I've-got-over-it tone, which would at least make sense to her. 'Along with my strategic forecast for the business for the upcoming couple of years.'

The hand she'd been waving around now hid itself in a fold of her sundress's knee-length skirt.

'Thanks.' Again his lips curved into that hint of a smile. 'I'll jump straight in.'

'I'd best get on with my work, too.' Cecilia dropped into her chair. 'I have invoices to get into the system from the weekend's trade.'

She did *not* mention that she'd spent so much time ensuring that the outdoor aspects of the nursery were impeccable in recent days that she'd allowed that invoicing to get somewhat behind.

She'd known Linc would be here and that he'd want her around—at least to start with. This way she could work while she answered any questions he might have.

That's right. You weren't hiding out doing your favourite tasks just because they help you not to think about other things.

Cecilia had a major event coming up for the nursery. She simply didn't have time to think about anything else. Not family stresses, not her abandonment by Hugh and certainly not this morning's odd noticing of Linc in a way she had stopped herself doing for years.

Cecilia jabbed the start button of her Slimline computer. 'I'll be here all day in the office to be sure I'm available for any questions you may have.'

'I appreciate that you're so well organised for the review, even with a big event looming on the horizon.'

Linc MacKay murmured the words as his plant-nursery manager shuffled her bottom into her office chair and peered down her nose at the computer screen in front of her.

She looked beautiful today…a summery woman with golden skin. Her shoulders were bare but for a couple of spaghetti straps on the deep red sundress splashed with a bold floral design, and her lips were highlighted in a subtle lipstick.

Linc had rejected her innocent overtures six years ago, even though he'd felt a spark of interest at the time. It had never truly gone away, and he had felt that fact keenly today. Seeing her in the beautiful sundress, showing such a feminine side of herself, Linc felt as though he were seeing her in a whole new light.

And because that awareness wasn't acceptable to him, he forced his focus to her business acumen.

Cecilia was determined and motivated and very capable when it came to running a nursery. Her push to gain a share in this one had impressed him, and she'd earned that opportunity over the last six years.

She was an intriguing woman, Linc acknowledged silently, and his glance returned to her once again.

Slender, with shoulder-length hair every shade from ash to dark blond and eyes the colour of bluebonnets…

Where had he been?

Right. Her inner strength and drive impressed him. Linc told himself not to think about how sweet she looked, how he felt as though layers had been pulled from his eyes and he could see her clearly for the very first time.

'I'll review the strategic projections first.' He pushed the knowledge of her appeal to the back of his mind, where it had to remain. 'Those will form a solid basis for the rest of my review. They'll also help me to spot any areas where the business might not yet be living up to its full potential.'

'I'll be keen to discuss any weak areas with you.' Cecilia sat very upright in her chair. 'I pride myself on trying to keep everything strong. I've printed a copy of the projections document for you.'

She pointed to the pile of files beside his computer. The document sat right on top.

'I appreciate it.' He lifted the sheaf of pages and flipped through them before turning back to the first page and lowering his gaze so he could fully concentrate on it.

It took a while, but Linc did immerse himself in the work. Even if he *could* see acres of soft, delicately sun-kissed skin in the periphery of his view.

Cecilia focused studiously on her office work, but out of the corner of her eye she remained very aware of Linc as the hours passed.

She wanted to know how he felt about his findings so far, even though he would have only just scratched the surface at this stage.

Distractingly, she noticed the scent of his aftershave. It made her think about things that had no business being in her mind.

'Cecilia?'

'Yes. No. I mean—' Had Linc asked her a question while she'd been daydreaming about woodsy scents and clear grey eyes? She had no idea—and no business noticing his eyes. Or his shoulders. Or the way his strong nose perfectly matched the firm, sensuous appeal of his lips.

Concentrate, Cee! On something other than how gorgeous he is.

'I might get a bite to eat.' He glanced at the clock on the wall. 'It's getting to be that time of day. Would you like to join me, or can I pick up something for you?'

For a moment blank incomprehension filled her. She fought her way out of it and realised she *was* hungry—but a lunch date with Linc MacKay...?

'Thanks, but I have errands to run on my lunch break.' Fortunately, his invitation had been offhand enough that she didn't need to worry about causing offence by refusing it.

Exactly.

So why had her heart skipped a beat?

'Plus, I brought something to eat from home.' Something dull and ordinary that held no uncertain surprises and certainly wouldn't make her think back to a past time when she had wanted to know Linc better on a personal rather than a business footing. 'But I appreciate the offer.'

He gave a little nod and a half smile and went on his way—which quite put it into perspective, as she should have done from the start. Thank goodness she hadn't sounded as though she were turning him down in a personal way or anything like that.

Cecilia ate her home-packed sandwich at her desk, and then headed for the nearby mall. Her thoughts turned to her sister more and more with each step. Hugh might have dropped Cecilia like the proverbial hot potato when her family life had suddenly gone from slightly troublesome to really concerning, and that still hurt, but it was the rift with Stacey that remained as a constant source of heartache any time Cecilia let the thoughts surface.

Rejection seemed to have formed a bit too much of a repeat cycle in Cecilia's life lately. It was just as well that she had learned to bury her emotions in her work and that she was very *good* at that work.

'Next, please.' The voice of the man behind the counter at the postal outlet drew her from her thoughts.

'Hello. I need to purchase a money order, please.'

'Same name and amount?'

The clerk probably thought he was being helpful, asking that. Instead, it just reminded Cecilia of how many times she had done this. Every Monday for the past five months, and it wasn't over yet.

Not this guy's fault, and not your fault, either, so smile and be normal. Got it?

She was fulfilling a duty, and if that felt like a paltry thing to do, well, the situation wasn't easy—and doing this was a lot more than just duty. She had to continue to hope that things would improve.

'Yes. Thank you.'

Cecilia placed the money order into a pre-stamped envelope and mailed it.

As she returned to work she let her spirits find happiness again. She loved the nursery and loved what she'd achieved here. And if she felt a little lift, knowing she was about to see Linc again, too, that came from knowing that every moment in his presence brought the results of the review and his decision about her share proposition closer. It was that and only that.

If she didn't entirely believe herself, Cecilia ignored the fact.

Her peace lasted until she approached the office and heard Linc speaking.

'I can tell you really want to speak with her, but Cecilia is at lunch just now.' There was a pause. 'Are you in a position where you could call back a bit later?'

'Is that for me? I'll take it now.' She could hardly speak for the buzzing in her ears, and she saw Linc was ending the call even as she spoke.

For a moment after he'd placed the phone back in its cradle, she simply stood there.

'That was a supplier wanting to change an order.'

Linc seemed to be searching her face with a great deal of attention.

It was just a supplier, phoning on the office phone. Your sister only has your cell phone number. You haven't missed a chance to speak with her, and Linc hasn't found out anything about her.

Disappointment and relief fought for supremacy inside Cecilia.

They both won.

'The guy sounded old...grumpy.' Linc gave a what-do-you-do kind of a shrug. 'He didn't want to leave his name or number, only wanted to speak with you, and he ended the call quite abruptly.'

'I think I know which supplier that would have been.' She walked to her desk, sat down. Felt Linc's gaze on her and an added layer of awareness of her that she would swear, despite her admonitions to herself earlier to the contrary, was real.

Did she want to set herself up for further rejection? No.

Exactly, Cecilia. So get your mind back on your work. Now!

But trying to do that just reminded her that her heart had almost stopped for a second or two, and now she was fighting a renewed sense of sadness and loss that she tried to keep distant during work hours.

'I'll call the supplier back a bit later and let him know that a message would be welcome the next time, whether I'm here or not.'

Next time she wouldn't practically fall apart over a silly, perfectly routine, office-related phone call.

Cecilia ignored the reasons why she *would* panic, and why she now felt deflated and sad all over again. Because no cause for panic had actually ensued. She'd ignored the way Linc had made her feel today so far, too. If she ignored that for long enough, she would get it under control.

She turned her attention back to her work. In the end, that was where her focus needed to stay!

CHAPTER TWO

'IS THERE A chance we could move my tour of the facility forward and do it now? I have to disappear for a while later this morning on other business.'

Linc made the request as he and Cecilia met at the front area of the plant nursery the next morning. They'd driven into the staff parking area within seconds of each other.

'I'm sorry for the disruption to our review, but would that be manageable for you?'

'There's no need to apologise. I'm surprised you got through even one day without a disruption, to be honest. And the flower show management team aren't due here until eleven—so, yes, I can do the tour now.'

Cecilia's words and tone were calm. Yet in catching her unawares Linc had glimpsed what had looked like sorrow in her eyes, before she'd shielded her expression and the mantle of 'business manager' came down over her face.

There'd been an awareness of him, too. It had sparked briefly before that mantle had come down. It disturbed him that he had looked and hoped for that very thing. And it disturbed him that she had seemed sad.

He frowned, but a moment later Cecilia spoke with such enthusiasm and apparent focus on her work that he wondered if he had imagined that earlier moment of interest and its preceding sadness.

'It'll be a real pleasure to show you everything here in detail. Just let me stow my things, Linc, and we'll get into the tour.'

Cecilia quickly divested herself of her purse and her lunch, tucked her cell phone into the back pocket of her jeans, and led the way to the first part of the nursery.

She'd been an intriguing young woman at twenty, when she'd fought so hard to get him to let her manage one of his nurseries. With nothing but a community college course and some time spent in customer service in a small plant nursery behind her, she'd gone after her dream of managing one, tenaciously.

Linc would have been a fool not to employ her, so he had done exactly that. But not before she had let him see that she would have welcomed the opportunity to know him better as a *man*, not only as a potential employer.

Her interest then hadn't been one-sided.

And now…?

Now, for his sins, Linc had seen a whole new aspect of her yesterday, and that had not only refreshed the underlying awareness of Cecilia that had never truly left him, but had added to it. *Why?* Was it because there'd been no woman in his life at all lately?

Well, he'd been busy.

Too busy to pick up the phone and invite someone out or to say yes to any of the invitations that came his way?

Was he getting jaded? Or perhaps lonely? Wanting what his brothers had in their marriages?

That last thought came out of nowhere, and Linc shoved it right back there just as quickly. Ridiculous. He was perfectly happy as he was. He ignored any possibility that he might not be.

Linc's gaze was focused on the back of Cecilia's head as she walked along a curved pathway ahead of him, but all that did was draw his attention to her again.

A yellow sleeveless shirt contrasted with denim cut-offs, and both highlighted her soft curves. Today she wore her hair up in that ponytail again, and it bounced with every step of her work-booted feet.

The ponytail made Linc want to kiss her, and while the sensible work attire spoke of her determination, she looked equally as appealing to Linc today as she had yesterday—all feminine curviness and beauty.

Layers had definitely been peeled from his eyes, and Linc wanted to paste them right back on. He needed to do that, because Cecilia wasn't the kind of woman he'd date and forget—the type of woman he had always dated because it was easy to walk away.

He had to set aside this awareness of Cecilia—whether he'd suddenly noticed her on a whole different level or not.

Cecilia glanced over her shoulder. 'Shall we visit the cold storage first?'

'Yes. That would be…ah…great.'

They headed over there, and Linc forced his attention back to the tour. He noticed the amount of empty space surrounding the limited offerings of cut flowers.

'How's the cut-flower trade going?'

'It's going well.'

Her glance seemed only to calculate the empty shelf area. But her cheeks held a hint of pink that couldn't be attributed to their brief walk.

Was she feeling this, too? This interest and curiosity that felt fresh and new and oh-so-tempting to pursue?

'At the moment we're keeping our stock orders tight.' She waved a hand in the general direction of the shelves, and then shoved it into the front pocket of her cut-offs.

She's as aware of it as you are.

Maybe, but that didn't mean she wanted to pursue it any more than he did, Linc reminded himself belatedly.

'Any special reason?' He cleared his throat. 'For keeping the stock orders tight?'

She tipped her head on one side and seemed to consider him for a moment before she responded. 'It's because Valentine's Day is very close and we'll need the space for all the cut roses.'

'Right. It's good that you've thought ahead to make as much of that day as possible.' His voice was so deep it might have come from his boots. 'I should have thought of that straight away.'

'It's a very special day.' The pink in her cheeks deepened. 'For—for the customers, and very much for the nursery.'

And most of all for lovers.

She didn't say that. Instead, she drew a deep breath, as though to try to compose herself.

In Linc's experience women seemed to expect a

very emotional expression of love on that particular day of the year. To show a love that encapsulated exactly the kind of commitment that would never be part of Linc's own life.

He was grateful his brothers had found such love—that their lives had turned out okay in the end. However, Linc would never deserve—

'We'll be getting in red roses, predominantly.'

Cecilia's words drew him back from the dark thoughts as she led the way out of the cold storage area and, once he'd joined her outside, secured it.

'We'll stock other colours of roses, too. There's a growing percentage of buyers who will purchase something other than the classic red—particularly when purchasing for friends or family rather than—'

'The romantic loves of their lives?'

There. He'd said it and the sky hadn't fallen in.

'Yes.' She glanced at him and quickly away again. Her chin tipped up. 'Roses are lovely at any time of the year. My favourites are the creamy white ones. They have a beautiful, subtle scent.'

She led the way through a section of potted seedlings and, as he came to her side, gave him the benefit of a determinedly work-focused gaze.

'Hopefully this year's sales of roses will prove to be as lucrative as last—if not more so.'

The words made Cecilia sound as unromantic as they came, and she *was* a great businesswoman. But one who'd managed to bring romance right to the heart of her working life through her instigation of this year's masked-ball event. Not to mention all the flowers she stocked for Valentine's Day, and the flowering maze she had designed and nurtured to fruition.

'Given your track record over the last six years, I have no doubt that the Valentine's Day trade will exceed all expectations.' He made the comment matter-of-fact, but his thoughts were not pragmatic.

She'd been in a relationship a few months ago. His brother Brent had mentioned that it had ended.

So she's single.

Why would Linc even consider her availability?

She may be hurting and still love the guy.

'Thank you.'

For a moment Linc didn't know what she was thanking him for, and then he remembered. He'd paid her a compliment. A business one, about her ability to do a great job as plant-nursery manager.

Which was true.

'You're welcome.'

They moved between rows of gardening supplies, through arrays of flowering plants and herbs, potting mix and foliage. Linc began to find his focus again, and the colour in Cecilia's cheeks returned to normal.

So it was fine. He'd been foolishly carried away—imagining things, nothing more. Flights of fancy weren't Linc's style. He would make sure it didn't happen again.

Cecilia's love of her work shone through more and more as she talked avidly, explaining the progress and plans that related to each area.

'What's happening in that shed?'

He asked the question as they walked towards a shady path, far into the back section of the nursery. Access to the shed was gained through a locked gate. There were no customers to be seen or heard, and it truly felt secluded and private.

In fact, it was the perfect setting for a man to steal a kiss. Assuming that a man would choose to do something so unprofessional.

So much for him returning his thoughts to nothing but business.

'I'll show you.' Cecilia led the way to this final shed on the property and unlocked and opened the door. The tour with Linc had proved productive so far, but she had been oh-so-conscious of him the entire time.

This sharpened interest towards Linc needed to stop.

She felt a moment of nervous anticipation as she prepared to reveal this part of the business. It was working well, and she was proud of it, but what would Linc think of the concept?

'I hope you'll approve of this aspect of the nursery.' She tried to imbue nothing but confidence into her tone as she went on. 'This is where I work on my repurposing projects. I get some of my best ideas for the future direction of the business when I'm working here, too.'

With this statement carefully delivered, and avoiding the thought that she also came here when she missed her sister the most, Cecilia glanced about the area.

Sunlight streamed through skylights in the roof into a large open-plan area that housed projects in various stages of completion. Old boots with creepers growing out of them...a rocking chair that had been painted orange and black, its seat area filled with a large planter of pumpkin vine... Demand for this kind of repurposed item was growing.

'I didn't know about this.' Linc's gaze moved about the area before it returned to her. 'How long have you been doing this work? Where did you get all these items?'

He wouldn't realise it, but the sun coming through the skylight above had cast his profile into sharp relief. Every strong feature and every subtle nuance was there for her to see. Right down to the length of his dark eyelashes and the way they curled slightly at the ends. And the shape of his lips…

Cecilia struggled to remember his question. He'd asked something about where she got the items for refurbishment. It was one of her favourite aspects of the plant nursery, which showed how easily being around Linc could throw her completely off her guard.

'I find items in all sorts of places.'

She took a step to the side, to break that particular view of him. It was as though she'd jumped back through time six years and all her past awareness of him as a man had returned.

Actually, it hadn't—because she saw him now with a history of working in his employ for six years. She saw him with more maturity. With more certainty in her interest in him…

'I started this operation about four months ago.'

Soon after she'd realised she needed a distraction and a way of letting out her emotions, thanks to the implosions going on in her personal life.

She simply *couldn't* feel a renewed attraction to Linc, let alone a deeper one. Because—because business and that sort of pleasure didn't mix. Because she had enough to deal with in her life without trying to take on a romance. Because she'd learned the hard way, when Hugh had disappeared from her life without a backward glance, that you just couldn't trust romantic attachments once 'real life' interfered with them!

Most of all because Linc had rejected her overtures all those years ago. *Remember?* There was no earthly reason why he'd feel any differently now.

'Any time I'm out and about I visit garage sales and junk shops…thrift stores and car boot sales.'

Perhaps if she made herself sound like a lonely single girl with a craft obsession, she would embarrass herself out of being so conscious of him.

'All the items are ridiculously cheap to buy,' she continued, 'and people leap at the chance to purchase the end product—the repurposed item. There's good profit to be made, and the items appeal to the style of visitor who comes here to tour the maze. Jemmie features them online, as well.'

His strong hands lifted a pottery urn from the bench. It had a chunk missing from one side. 'So a buyer will pay top dollar for this?'

'Once the urn has herbs growing in it, or maybe some flowering cacti, you'll be surprised how quickly it will be snapped up.'

She took the urn from his hands, held it up to the light. She ignored her fanciful thoughts and how it felt to stand so close to him, to measure her smaller frame against his taller, stronger one.

Get over it, Cee. Get over it right now!

Cecilia went on to tell Linc about her repurposing timetable, and then led the way back through the nursery acreage to the maze, quickly showing Linc the upgrades she'd had done to the *fruticetum* at the centre of it. Its circular arrangement combined colourful blooming potted shrubs with evergreen native species.

'Clever work.' He made the declaration the moment they stepped into the central area. 'Those shrubs grouped all around the edges of the circular space will add to the air of mystery for the masked ball.'

She gestured to the picnic tables dotted around the central area as well as the edges.

'Currently, when folks finish touring the maze, they can sit for a while, enjoy the quiet and utilise the screens embedded in the tabletops to scroll through our available stock lists and place orders. They can either take them with them, collect later or have them sent to any address they choose. The night of the ball there'll be a raised dais for dancing. The central picnic tables will be shifted out to the edges of the area and the canopied dais will be assembled on-site the day before the event.'

Something she had told herself was mostly about commerce and exposure for the business suddenly felt quite personal to Cecilia. She could imagine herself on that dais, dancing with a handsome partner.

Well, a girl could buy into a romantic idea, couldn't she? Even if it *was* an idea she had germinated to increase the popularity of her business.

As for that vision of herself on the dais... The man who appeared in it with her looked remarkably like Linc.

Heat warmed the back of her neck. The middle of a working tour was not the time for such flights of fancifulness. Hadn't she allowed herself to be distracted enough by him this morning?

'Will it be an old-fashioned ball?' he queried. 'With waltzing and so on?'

Was his voice deeper than usual? Cecilia glanced at his face but couldn't read his expression.

'There will be waltzes and other simpler dance tunes. I want people at all levels of dancing ability to be able to participate,' she murmured, and then had to clear her throat and strive for a stronger tone. 'I hope to create a night to remember.'

His gaze met hers and, for one breathless moment, electricity seemed to charge the air between them.

'I'm sure you'll achieve that.'

Oh, Linc, do you feel this too?

'I hope you'll be there.' The words came unthinkingly, and the warmth that had started at the back of her neck now rushed into her cheeks.

Had she not learned the last time?

She rushed on. 'What I mean is, it would look good to have the owner here. For business. But I understand you may be busy. It's not an expectation.'

Cecilia *had* asked the question with business in mind. She had!

'I'll have to consider—' He broke off as his cell phone started to ring.

Yet not before Cecilia sensed the hesitation in him.

So there. That answered her unspoken question.

Of *course* he wouldn't want to involve himself in a masked ball. She had never asked him to do anything like that before. Why should she start now?

Mortification threatened, because she did *not* want him to see her request as an overture. It didn't matter what she might or might not have felt towards him since his arrival to undertake this review of the business.

Her request had been about *business*, and she needed Linc to know that.

Cecilia ignored the little voice that suggested it had been a little bit about the man himself, as well...

A moment later he'd responded briefly to the caller. He turned to Cecilia. 'I'm sorry. That was the call I've been waiting on. I need to go.'

'You're fine. Go do what you need to do.' Cecilia waved him away as though she had some claim to granting him permission or not. 'And don't worry about my invitation. I understand if you can't make it or don't want to attend. It was a marketing-related thought. That's all.'

Another thought encroached. What if he *did* attend the masked ball and arrived with some beautiful woman on his arm?

Not her business—and she wouldn't care one way or the other!

Linc gave a quick nod and strode off.

Cecilia did *not* watch his departure until he was out of sight, nor did she stand there daydreaming, incapable of remembering what she should do next even though she'd just given herself a stern internal talking-to.

She merely took a moment to gather herself for her next job. Yes. That was what she did.

And that job needed to be a last-minute check of the maze before the flower-show committee arrived.

Cecilia forced her attention to her work. And it was as she inspected the perfect flowerbeds that Cecilia admitted to herself that she really did hope Linc would attend the masked ball.

But only for business purposes.

'You can go ahead and sell off two of the three apartment complexes as whole lots to those investors. It's a good time to do it, and you know the profit margin I'll be looking for.'

Linc gave his agreement over his cell phone to his property broker as he strode from his car to the entrance of Cecilia's plant nursery the following morning.

'The third is to be offered as individual units under the first home-buyer arrangement we have with our partner real estate firms.'

'You know that plan is neither time efficient nor as cost-effective as the investor option.' His broker's voice held the tone of an oft-repeated lament.

Linc treated the warning to the same response he gave it every time. 'Nevertheless, you know where I stand on this.'

'There are times when you're going to give back, whether it reduces your profit margin or not. Yeah, I know. I'm proof of that myself.' The other man gave a wry laugh and yielded the point. 'You gave *me* a great chance when you employed me, and I haven't looked back since.'

'You can fill the time while you're waiting for those units to sell by property shopping for me in Queensland,' Linc offered. 'How does that sound? I've been wanting to buy into that state for a while.'

He gave his broker—suddenly a much happier

man—his instructions, ended the call and set out to find Cecilia.

'She's in the office.' Jemmie, Cecilia's second-in-command, told him as Linc strode across the court-yard.

'Thanks.'

As Linc headed for the office, he acknowledged silently that he really *wanted* to see Cecilia. He *should* want to see her again to prove to himself that this recent and inexplicable sharpening of his interest in her had disappeared as quickly as it had made its presence felt.

Odd that he should feel a lift in his spirits as he approached the door of the plant-nursery office, if that was the case.

The office door stood open. As Linc drew closer, observing Cecilia's concentration and hearing the sound of her voice as she spoke into the phone, he silently acknowledged that she looked beautiful sitting there and that seeing her gave him a warm, happy feeling.

He could live with that without ever doing a thing about it. In a short span of time he'd be out of here and back to his regular world, anyway.

Out of the way of temptation?

'Linc. Hi.' She glanced up after ending her call and offered a welcoming smile.

For a moment Cecilia looked equally happy to see him. Happy and...*interested*? Linc couldn't take his gaze from hers. And blue eyes stared back at him—before she seemed to realise how long their glances had held.

She dropped her gaze. 'I wasn't sure if you'd be here today.'

He stepped over the threshold and let his gaze linger on her face, enjoying the lovely lines, the sweep of her lashes against her cheeks.

'The business with my property guy didn't take long.' Linc gave himself full points for sounding so close to normal. 'I wound it up a few minutes ago on the phone, actually.'

He brushed aside his travelling all over Sydney to inspect his property holdings as though it had barely impinged. Right now it didn't seem to matter. All he could focus on was Cecilia.

What the heck was going on with him?

'Besides, I've got this review to do for you. It still shouldn't take too long if I get a good run at it.'

As though to mock him, his phone rang.

'I think you may have spoken too soon.' Amusement crinkled the skin at the corners of Cecilia's eyes, and her mouth turned up into a soft smile.

Linc lost himself in her in that moment. His breath caught and, still stuck on that smile, he answered his phone absent-mindedly.

He had to run the caller's first few words back through his mind again before he could focus. 'Sorry, Alex. Which export law did you say is concerning you?'

Linc forced his attention to the call.

Cecilia turned her focus to her work while Linc spoke on the phone with his brother. It felt strangely intimate to be in the same room with Linc while he did that, yet she had learned from his brief time here so far that he would step outside if he wanted privacy for a call.

Maybe she should find a reason to step out, anyway. She didn't need to add any extra feelings of intimacy to her connection with this man. She was having enough trouble ignoring her awareness of him as it was.

She started to stand.

'Okay. Tell Jayne I said hi.' Linc's voice softened noticeably as he said his goodbyes on the phone. 'I'll stop by to see you both tonight on my way home.'

The man loved his family to pieces.

Cecilia's heart softened and ached a little at one and the same time. He must be close to his family. That was so appealing. Yet it made her feel sad because she, on the other hand, was experiencing a difficult phase with her sister.

But that was going to get better. It *was*!

Linc ended the call and glanced up just as Cecilia settled back into her chair. 'How did the committee's visit go yesterday?'

'It went well.' She welcomed the distraction from her thoughts more than he could know. 'The committee members were happy with the standard of the maze and with the area that will be used at its centre for dancing. There will only be a hundred guests. Tickets to the ball are being auctioned online, with proceeds going to charity. I'm relieved the committee were satisfied with my plans and with the site itself.'

If the nursery played its cards right, it might get a yearly event out of this. She would definitely hold more balls for special occasions…weddings. The possibilities were endless. Cecilia couldn't help but feel a little excited about the doors this first event might open up.

'It sounds as though you have things well under control.' Linc murmured the words as he sat down to recommence his review.

Cecilia laughed. She didn't mean to, but the sound escaped her. 'All except the fact that Valentine's Day is about to erupt onto my work horizon, whether I feel ready for it or not—and I'm leaning somewhat towards the "not" side of that particular equation right now.'

As Linc turned his attention to his work—with numerous interruptions on his cell phone, despite his desire for a clear run at the review—Cecilia refocused and settled in to finalise stock orders for Valentine's Day.

She worked hard, but she had to admit—to herself, at least—that Linc's proximity was corroding her concentration. He was just so *there*.

And she was so busy. Every time she tried to work on her orders, the phone rang again or a supplier called through directly on her cell phone. There were cancellations of previously established orders, stockists informing her that they'd oversold to other buyers and couldn't fill *her* order, asking if other blooms could be substituted.

Cecilia's answer was always the same. No, they couldn't!

This happened every year—it was part of dealing with this particular day on the nursery's calendar—but that didn't make it any less busy or any less challenging for her to ensure she reached her necessary stock levels.

On top of that the floor staff came in more often than usual, with odd questions that simply couldn't wait. The more that time passed, the busier it became.

'Linc, I'm putting this call on speaker. I'm sorry if it disturbs your concentration.'

She tried not to let frustration colour her tone as she jabbed at the settings on her cell phone. Once she had placed it atop the filing cabinet in the corner of the room, she began to riffle through the cabinet's contents.

'It's fine. I can see you're under pressure.'

Linc's words were calm. He had fielded numerous distractions of his own since he got here today, and he seemed quite unfazed. As though he didn't find Cecilia's presence and nearness at all disturbing.

Not that Cecilia felt agitated due to *his* presence. Certainly not in any personal kind of way. She'd had that conversation with herself earlier. She simply had to get over the nerve-racking, overalert, oh-so-conscious of him feeling.

And she was over it. She 100 per cent totally *was*. Her consciousness could just catch up with that attitude right now!

'Mr Sampson, I have your previous delivery docket, your invoice and a receipt showing a nil balance in front of me.' She gave the reference number, speaking towards her phone. 'If funds are outstanding to your company, they aren't owed from here.'

After a moment the man discovered a mistake at

his end. He agreed to finalise Cecilia's order for the next day and ended the call.

With Mr Sampson sorted out, Cecilia replaced the file in the cabinet and returned to her desk.

Time passed. And when a customer phoned with a special request for a particular style of repurposed item, and Cecilia happened to be able to match it, she decided to take the opportunity to head to the repurposing shed to collect the piece.

She replaced the desk phone in its cradle. 'You'll be okay for a few minutes, Linc? I'll put the phone through to Jemmie, out front.'

'Leave it. I believe I may *just* be able to manage without you for a little bit without having to disturb Jemmie.'

His wry smile brought out every gorgeous manly feature. It also undid every bit of Linc-ignoring effort Cecilia had put in today.

Before she could stop herself, she smiled back. A big, wide, pleased-with-the-world smile that brushed across her face and made Linc grow still before an enigmatic veil came down over his eyes.

Her breath hitched, and just like that it was all there again. The awareness. The *interest.*

She drew in a slightly shaky inhalation. 'Okay. I'll…ah… I'll leave the phone. I'd better go take care of this.'

Before she did something she regretted for the *second* time since knowing him.

Cecilia exited the office and gave herself a good talking-to while she was at it. She wasn't interested in Linc. Such an interest wasn't something she could allow to exist. Just because her boyfriend had dumped her when her issues with her sister had hit crisis point, it didn't mean she should try to pick up the next available—

Oh, get over yourself, Cecilia. And get over Hugh, too.

As if Linc would participate in that possibility, anyway. He was a millionaire, for crying out loud, *so* successful in life. *And* he'd already rejected her once before. Was she trying to line herself up for a second shot at that humiliation?

She wasn't. She just hadn't expected to feel this attraction to and interest in Linc again. It had surprised her. All she needed to do was adjust to that surprise factor and she would be fine.

In minutes she was back at the office.

'Item retrieved and left with the front staff ready for collection.' She spoke as she stepped over the threshold of the office space.

'Great.' Linc was in the process of putting down the office phone extension as he responded. 'I've taken a couple of messages. You'll know what to do with them.'

He didn't break into a big smile. She didn't, either. That earlier moment of blinding connection had passed. So why could she still not seem to be able to tear her gaze from him? And why did he gaze so intently at her? And had she not taken any notice whatsoever of her earlier warnings to herself?

Immersed in those thoughts, she was slow to realise that her cell phone had started to ring.

When she did realise it, she barely gave the caller's identity a thought. It would be some supplier again. However, she wasn't sure where her phone actually was.

Cecilia patted her pockets. Her gaze searched the desk. Then, without any warning whatsoever, the worst possible thing happened for her privacy, and perhaps the most heart-wrenching yet hope-inspiring thing for her emotions.

The phone's voicemail picked up automatically, went straight on to the speaker setting she'd left it on and a tinny prerecorded message from the caller's end began to play out into the room.

'Are you willing to accept a call from the Fordham Women's Correctional Centre? Your sister, Stacey Tomson, wishes to speak with you... '

The revealing words blared across the room as though trumpeted through a megaphone by the world's largest elephant.

'If you do not want to accept this call—'

She'd left the phone on the filing cabinet. She had received only two other calls like this, and questions filled her mind.

Why had Stacey chosen now to phone? Did it mean their rift might be ending or would they argue again?

So many emotions swirled inside Cecilia in that moment. Hurt. Frustration. Disappointment. Love.

Cecilia quickly crossed the room, grabbed up the phone and fumbled to take it off speaker.

One glance at Linc's face told her it was way too late to try and hide this, but she managed to change the setting and get the phone to her ear. She wasn't sure if he'd heard her sister's voice or not, but when she started towards the door, to leave the room, it was to realise Linc had beaten her to it.

The door clicked shut behind his receding back, and Cecilia could acknowledge both the joy and the pain of finally receiving this call when she hadn't known when or even *if* she ever would.

She said hello to her troubled, incarcerated twin.

CHAPTER THREE

'STACEY. HOW ARE YOU? I've been hoping you'd call. It's so hard not being allowed to call you. It's been such a long time. I've missed you so!'

Are you still angry that I said you needed to change your direction in life? I wanted to help you, and it needed to be said!

Cecilia didn't want the gap between them to widen even more, and yet if she hadn't challenged Stacey, who would have?

The man who'd disappeared and left Stacey to carry this punishment alone? Who'd appeared to do nothing but manipulate Cecilia's sister up to that point?

'Are you okay?'

She couldn't make herself say *Are you okay in jail?* Or even, *Are you okay in there?*

'Have you been getting the money orders for extra food and things?'

'Yes, I've been getting them.'

Cecilia thought she heard Stacey swallow hard before her sister went on.

'Thank you for doing that.'

'You're my sister.' Emotion rose in Cecilia's throat.

'Cee, I wanted to ask if you'd be willing to start visiting me again.' Stacey's words couldn't mask her emotion. 'I've missed you. I should have called sooner. I was angry, and it's tough in here. There's been a lot of adjusting to do—'

'Of course I'll visit again. I've been dying to see you.' So much relief coursed through Cecilia that she wanted to laugh and cry at once. 'We can talk about your future, when you're finally out of there.'

Surely that would be something they could both look forward to?

'We can.' Stacey sounded on the verge of tears before she spoke again. 'I don't want to not be talking to you. I guess I felt hurt at a time when I needed you to just love me. But there's been time for me to think, and to realise I've made some really big mistakes.'

'I'm really sorry, Stacey.'

Cecilia had thought she was doing the right thing in pointing out the bad pathway that Stacey had followed. For some reason she'd thought that because Stacey had been so angry at the time her sister couldn't possibly have been hurting. Tears sprang to the backs of Cecilia's eyes again. How could she have been so short-sighted?

'I should have found a better way to deal with your situation than I did.'

'You were worried about me, and with good reason.' Stacey sighed. 'I can't understand now how I was so blind. Joe seemed nice at first—a little rough around the edges, but charming with it.'

'And then the charm wore off.' Cecilia understood that. She'd been there herself with Hugh. At least in this she could try to rebuild some solidarity with her sister. 'We're not very good at finding great men, are we?'

Stacey agreed, and then sounded a little troubled and vulnerable as she went on. 'I need to tell you that if you start coming to see me it will help my chances of gaining parole, because I'll be demonstrating that I have a sound relationship with someone reliable. I want you to know that before you come in, so you don't think I asked just because of it. I've missed you and I'm longing to see you.'

'I believe you, and I want that sound relationship again.' Cecilia had longed for it over the past months. 'I'm so glad you phoned, Stacey.'

'I am, too. I'm *allowed* to have a sister.' Stacey's words were firm, almost defiantly so. '*And* to see you and have a relationship with you. I should have stuck up for that from the start.'

'Of course you are.' Cecilia frowned. 'Who's told you otherwise? Surely not the authorities there?'

'Joe did—constantly throughout my relationship with him and again quite recently before I finally woke up.'

Cecilia clamped her teeth together so she wouldn't speak without thinking first. Finally, she said carefully, 'I thought that after the armed robbery he'd gone underground. Wouldn't he be detained and taken in by the police if he visited you?'

'He found a way to get messages to me in here through another inmate who was about to be released.' Stacey admitted it in a low voice. 'At first I was happy. I thought there must be some explanation for Joe dragging me into what happened that day and then leaving me to pay for being an accomplice to something

I didn't even understand was going to happen until it was too late.'

'I'm guessing that's not what happened?' Cecilia wished she could give her sister a hug.

'No. He wanted me to tell him if I had any secret money stashed anywhere outside of here or any valuable jewellery.' Stacey made a disgusted sound. 'I sent a message back telling him never to contact me again.'

'That was horrible of him, Stacey.' Cecilia could only be glad that Stacey had cut the man off. 'I love you, sis. We've got through life up to this point, and we can keep getting through it.' Cecilia struggled not to choke up again. 'I just want to see you. When can I come?'

'Let me talk to the officers here and find out.' Relief filled Stacey's tone.

'You'll ring again?' Cecilia wanted that assurance before Stacey hung up.

'I will. As soon as I know when you can come.'

They said their goodbyes then, and Cecilia slowly placed the phone into her pocket. They'd never been cut off from each other before. At least now she could see Stacey. Relief and gratitude tugged even further at her teetering emotions.

But right now, somewhere on the other side of the door, Cecilia had to face Linc. What could he possibly think?

Stacey had been unhappy since they were teenagers, but this was the first time she had done anything actually against the law. No one knew about the jail sentence. In fact, no one here had even met Stacey. The sisters had tended to meet up after work, and then when Joe had come on the scene, Stacey had kept contact with Cecilia to a minimum. Cecilia understood why now.

The guy hadn't wanted anyone else to have influence in Stacey's life. Thank goodness her sister had finally sent the man packing.

Cecilia wanted to undo Stacey's history and get her out of there because she'd been tricked. Those wishes were unrealistic, and she knew it, but she hated it that Stacey's life had been impacted so deeply by this whole situation.

Well, for now it was time to face Linc. Cecilia didn't feel ready, but she had no choice.

She forced herself to open the office door and to speak to Linc, who lounged with pseudocasualness against a pillar partway across the courtyard.

'I've finished my call. Thanks for giving me privacy for that.'

'It was no problem.' He started towards her.

Cecilia didn't know what else he might have said. Anything, or nothing at all. But suddenly she couldn't stay there to find out. Not right now. Not until she could get her emotions under better control. If he was sympathetic she might fall apart. She couldn't let that happen.

'I need to do a few things in the repurposing shed.' She blurted the words and turned on her heel. 'I'll be back in a bit.'

She couldn't even speak to him about getting Jemmie to come out of the retail section and cover the office during her absence. Cecilia couldn't say anything more at all. But she had her back turned before Linc reached her, and she walked herself quickly far enough into the rear of the nursery that no one would see her until she could blink back the well of emotion that threatened to overcome her.

It wasn't perfect. She shouldn't walk out on a busy office. But she needed time to gather herself.

Cecilia walked on and set to work on regaining her control—because that was what she needed to do.

Linc wanted to go after Cecilia. To ensure that she was okay. Although clearly he couldn't ensure any such thing, because she wasn't. The heartbreak she must have tried so hard to shore up before she opened the door minutes ago had been etched on her face.

That had shouted more loudly than any voice could have done for her to be given privacy to regroup. Even so, it had taken all his resources not to stride across the courtyard and take her into his arms.

She had a sister.

That sister was in a correctional facility.

Linc hadn't known either of those things.

What had Cecilia's sister done to land her where she was now? How long had Cecilia been trying to cope with this reality?

'Linc, I could use your help.'

The request from Cecilia's second-in-command forced his attention back to his surroundings, to the busy plant-nursery office. He'd called in Jemmie to help out, and the phone still kept ringing. The rest of the world remained unaware of Cecilia's turmoil and wasn't about to grant any concessions.

Jemmie went on. 'Will Cecilia be gone long? I've got an enquiry about one of her orders, and the amount of money involved is too substantial for me to make the judgment call alone. Unless *you* want to decide, Linc?'

'She won't be gone much longer.' Linc would have to go and find Cecilia before he let much more time pass. 'What exactly is the problem, Jemmie? I may be able to resolve it.'

He did just that, but he had no sense of satisfaction—only a gnawing awareness of the passage of time.

Linc frowned, checked his wristwatch again and got to his feet.

As he did so Cecilia stepped into the office space.

'Thanks for helping out, Jemmie.' She spoke as though nothing were amiss. 'You can head back now.'

The office phone rang. Cecilia answered it as Jemmie left. Again, Cecilia's composure seemed rock solid.

Except she was pale, her beautiful eyes looked as though she'd been crying and she wouldn't fully meet his gaze.

Linc waited while Cecilia took the call. When it had ended, he spoke carefully. 'I didn't know you had a sister.' He hoped that by acknowledging this in some way he might help Cecilia to feel less uncomfortable. 'I'm sorry that I heard the start of your conversation. If I'd known—'

'Stacey is my twin.' She searched his gaze. 'I wouldn't have expected you to know anything. This whole situation has been…challenging.'

'I can imagine.' Linc took care to allow that search and to keep his expression as open as possible. Cecilia might feel comfortable enough to confide in him a little more—not because he harboured some morbid curiosity about her difficulties, but because he cared.

He refused to ask himself whether that kind of care should fall within the realms of an employee/employer relationship. It fell within *his* realm.

After a moment Cecilia simply said, 'We hadn't spoken for months. We went through a really bad patch. Both of us were partly to blame, but I—I can see now that I let her down, and I regret that so much. Today was the start of turning that around, at least.'

'I'm happy for you—that there's a chance for you to get things on a better footing with your sister.' His words emerged in a deep tone. Linc hadn't managed to be there for his brothers when they had needed him vitally. For Alex most of all. He'd never forgiven himself for what he'd allowed to happen. His heart squeezed for Cecilia.

He cleared his throat. 'If there's anything—'

'Thank you.' She spoke quickly and seemed to force herself to draw a slow, deep breath. 'There's nothing. And it's busy.' She turned to her computer. 'I should get on with this work.'

Linc conceded to her need to refocus her attention and did the same, but her situation and his own memories from the past remained in his thoughts.

He'd hated the orphanage so much—the discipline and the emotional darkness and the complete lack of love or hope. Alex and Brent had saved him—had given him their brotherhood and let him love them and be loved in return.

Except at one vital point in time when Linc had failed in that charter.

And for that he could not forgive himself.

Linc forced his attention back to his review.

He still wanted to take Cecilia in his arms, but today's revelations had only drawn more attention to the reasons why he must let go of just such thoughts.

He wasn't worthy of her.

He never could be.

CHAPTER FOUR

'LINC. I WASN'T sure if I'd see you today.'

It was the following morning—Valentine's Day—and Cecilia had arrived at the nursery well ahead of schedule. She had wanted to be certain everything was in order for this most lucrative day on the nursery's calendar.

She had wanted time to compose herself before facing Linc again, if he did come in today, but would that composure even be possible? Yesterday's phone call with her sister had brought joy. That was undeniable. But it had also left Cecilia feeling exposed.

Yet when she searched Linc's gaze now, she saw only acceptance and, as their gazes held, awareness.

Cecilia stood on the outside of her office space, and Linc stood on the inside. She tried to pull herself back to the conversation. 'Did you—did you resolve your business challenge so soon?'

Linc had received a call from his brother late yesterday afternoon and had excused himself to go and take care of whatever matter had arisen.

'The problem was a joint investment I have with Alex.' The words were gruff. 'I'm sorry I left so abruptly yesterday. I had to deal with it quickly otherwise Alex could have lost a sizeable chunk of his portfolio. It is sorted out now.'

'I'm glad everything turned out okay.' She was, but her emotions were still a jumble. 'I had better print yesterday's orders, ready to start checking stock.'

Cecilia grasped the edge of the door and prepared to push it wider so she could enter.

'Actually, I hoped we could talk.' As he spoke those words he, too, reached for the door.

For long, still moments Cecilia felt the touch of warm, strong fingers over hers. *Linc's* fingers.

Aside from a handshake, when she'd first met Linc for her initial job interview, they'd never touched. But now they were, and that one simple touch undermined the slim control she'd had over her seesawing emotions—and over her attraction to Linc.

She wanted to know him better...to explore that interest. Now—today—she felt this. She hadn't shaken off that old interest in him at all. It had lain in waiting, ready to ambush her for a second time. It was a shock to admit that to herself, and as she searched his eyes, she wondered if those thoughts were reflected in hers.

'Cecilia...' Grey eyes searched her face, and his head dipped closer.

Her lips parted and her breath sighed out in a soft exhalation. She leaned towards him, just a little...

In the next moment, shocked at her own lack of control, she pulled back. How *could* she have ended up standing there with her emotions churning, so in need of his kiss?

Would he truly have kissed her? Had that been his intention?

A peek at his face revealed a mixture of surprise and...guilt?

Then his dark brows drew down, and she couldn't see into his eyes any more.

'Today—today will be manic.' She felt rather frenzied herself. Worked up. Freaked out.

You simply touched hands with him. Pull it together, Cecilia!

And he'd wanted to talk. About her sister phoning? About Stacey being in a women's prison?

Cecilia did *not* want to talk about that.

And now they'd almost kissed, and she needed to think about that—to figure out how she felt about that and why, if she'd interpreted it correctly, he should feel guilt over that.

'Delivery trucks will be arriving, and it won't stop after that.'

No sooner had she uttered the words than a truck could be heard, backing up to the loading bay.

The driver leaned on the horn.

The office phone began to jangle.

Linc frowned.

Cecilia raised her hands, palms up, towards him. 'It's Valentine's Day. The customers deserve their happiness. I can't deliver on that if I have to—'

'You're right. Now isn't the time.'

Linc conceded to Cecilia's declaration. He shouldn't have tried to bring up yesterday's shock revelation now, anyway.

But that moment in the doorway, when their hands had touched. He'd wanted to kiss her. He almost *had* kissed her.

Linc operated with a lot more self-control than that in life. He didn't get affected by *hand touching*.

So what was going on with him?

'I'll help out today, if it's going to be frantic. The review work can wait.'

'Th-thank you. I hope that won't be necessary, but I appreciate the offer.'

Her relief was heartfelt. Not because he'd offered to help out, Linc imagined, for he knew she could manage just fine without him and had done so for years. Her relief was patently because he'd backed off on his desire for an in-depth conversation. Who could blame her? If the roles were reversed, would *he* want to talk about it?

Or was her relief because that awkward moment in the doorway had ended?

He waved his hand in the direction of the truck. 'You get that. I'll take care of the phone.'

Apparently, the moment had been saved by the ring of the telephone and a truck full of red roses. For now, at least.

'So how's my brother enjoying this business review?' Brent MacKay asked the question cheerfully while well-ordered chaos reigned all around. 'I have to admit I was surprised when you told me you're thinking of giving Cecilia a share in the business. You've only ever taken on business partnerships with family up to this point.'

'It wouldn't be a gift. She's more than earned it in hard work over the past six years.'

It was later that day. The brothers stood in the busy nursery courtyard.

Linc watched Cecilia stride across the other side of it with a customer at her side and several more trailing at her heels like lovelorn ducklings.

'The review is progressing nicely.'

Except perhaps for today, when all he'd done was watch Cecilia rush to and fro while he'd fielded phone calls and observed the madness and the mayhem.

He'd taken care of some customers as well, to help share the load.

'And Cecilia's different. I'd be comfortable having a shared holding with her.'

Brent's eyebrows lifted. 'Oh, yes? Any reason in particular for that?'

Conversely, Linc's brows lowered. 'Because she's a trustworthy manager, and owning a share of the business would only make her more so.'

Linc started towards the nursery exit, where Brent had his utility truck parked out front.

'You *could* sound happier about that.' A corner of Brent's mouth turned up. He'd drawn level with Linc as they passed through the nursery exit. 'Anyway, I thought you'd be happy to see all this profit occurring right before your eyes—today at least?'

'I am.'

Of course Linc was. Any business owner would be pleased to see money coming in. Unless that owner didn't care just at the moment, because all he wanted to do was take the manager of the business aside and slow her down long enough to—

To do what? Talk to her about yesterday's startling revelation of her sister's situation, when he'd already had to concede that it wasn't the time to have that conversation?

Cecilia had made it pretty clear she didn't want any such discussion at *all* and that no time would be the right time for her.

Is that what you feel miffed about, MacKay? Or is it because she recoiled from that moment your hands touched at the door as though her fingernails were on fire?

It wasn't, either.

Fine—it was both.

Blast it. He didn't know!

'Is there anything else you need while you're here, Brent?' He slung the final bird's-nest fern into the back of his brother's utility truck and turned.

'Another one of those that *hasn't* just had half its foliage knocked off would be a start. I'm quite particular about the standard of plants that go into my landscape garden designs.' Brent said the words in a dry tone.

'Ah, sorry.' Linc glanced at the thing. 'I can replace that.'

'Don't worry. I've got enough to do without it if I have to.' Brent clapped him on the back.

'Did you know Cecilia has a twin sister? Or a sister at all, for that matter?' The words passed through Linc's lips before he could stop them.

Brent was halfway into the driver's seat of his truck. He settled fully and turned a quizzical gaze Linc's way. 'No. Why?'

'I didn't, either.'

How could he have known Cecilia for so long and not know the first thing about her personal life? He'd let her into *his* life. She knew his brothers. She'd been to their warehouse home a couple of times on business matters back when they had all lived there. She'd met Brent's and Alex's wives here at the plant nursery when they'd come shopping for things.

That was a lot of 'letting in' for a man who held his personal matters as close to his chest as Linc did.

He ignored the knowledge of all the things he *hadn't* let Cecilia in about—such as his entire personal life aside from her interactions with his family, most of which had been instigated by those family members rather than Linc himself, if he were honest about it.

Not the point. He hadn't deliberately shut Cecilia out of any of it.

She wasn't trying to shut you out, either, MacKay.

Linc didn't wait for Brent to respond. What could his brother say other than to ask him if he was feeling okay or had received a blow to the back of the head or something? Linc didn't know what to make of his own thoughts, anyway.

He saw Brent off and went back to helping out around the nursery. Sooner or later this romantic day would end. Maybe then he'd finally be able to focus on getting the review done, and then getting out of here and on with his life again.

The thought should have cheered him, but instead it made him feel unsettled and restless.

At the end of the day Linc found Cecilia in one of the auxiliary sheds, sweeping up rose petals. Although the room was empty now, except for those remnants, the scent of roses still filled the air.

'I thought I might find you here. The rest of the staff have gone home.' He'd come to find her and encourage her to leave. 'You should stop. You've pushed yourself hard today.'

His gaze tracked over her, registering the exhaustion stiffening her shoulders, the faint bruises beneath her eyes. A single deep red petal had caught in her hair.

'I wanted to get everything tidied up before I left.' The broom stilled in her hands as she looked up at him. Her face softened, and a weary pleasure lifted the corners of her mouth. 'We sent a lot of people home happy today, at least.'

In this moment she seemed to have found a true and deep contentment that came purely from wearing herself to the bone in order to *give*. Linc couldn't have admired her more.

'*You* did.' He took the remaining steps to her side and gently retrieved the broom from her hold. He placed it against a pillar.

'You contributed, Linc.' Her words were unguarded. 'I saw you helping out that little old lady who wanted roses for all her children and grandchildren.'

He *had* done that and, in amongst the antsy feelings he hadn't understood, Linc had found pleasure in giving that assistance.

But so much more had he admired Cecilia's generosity in doing the same, regardless of her personal circumstances. And now, in her presence, some of his restlessness today distilled into what it had really been. The need for her company, her attention, to focus on her and be with her. He couldn't explain the feelings. He already knew he had to stay away from her. And yet here he was.

Maybe if he tested this interest in her he would

prove to himself that the feelings were no different from those he'd felt towards any other woman who'd passed through his life. Then he could move on.

It was either sound reasoning or the flimsiest excuse of all time. Linc didn't try to discern which.

'There's just one petal remaining.' He reached up, drew the soft velvety petal from Cecilia's golden hair and placed it into her palm.

'Oh.' Her fingers closed over the petal. Her gaze lifted and searched his.

That was all. Just a touch and a glance and he was lost.

'I've wanted—' He searched *her* face, her eyes, and when he found curiosity, consciousness, he kissed her.

The moment their lips met, hers softened.

Oh, so sweetly.

Linc drew their joined hands to his chest and held them there. He wanted to keep kissing her and never stop. He wanted this one moment to last forever so he didn't have to think about it, or about what it meant, why it felt different from any kiss that had gone before it. Why his arms seemed to need so very much to envelop her. Instead, his fingers tightened around hers.

Cecilia had waited for Linc's kiss. She didn't want to admit that to herself, but it was true. She had wanted and needed to know how this would make her feel, and now she was experiencing it.

Against their joined hands she could feel the warmth of Linc's chest through his shirt, the hard wall of muscle. Yet his lips were soft as they caressed hers. She felt cherished and as if she was the absolute focus of his attention in this moment. She felt...*dif-*

ferent inside. As though this was changing her even as it happened.

Oh, she didn't want this kiss to end.

Cecilia curved her other hand against the column of his neck and acknowledged that this was not like it had been with Hugh. This was not like anything or anyone before.

Uncertainty rose then—because how could this touch her emotions so immediately? With this man who dated but didn't seem to look for the same kind of relationship as Cecilia did? The long-term, permanent kind?

'Cecilia...' Linc murmured her name against the side of her face as his lips left hers. He enveloped her in a hug.

She felt again the magnitude of the barriers within herself, wanting so very much to let them topple and fall, to open her heart to at least the hope of him.

Oh, Cecilia. That would be such foolishness. A kiss is a kiss is a kiss. With a man like Linc, how can you believe it means anything beyond the moment?

Hugs weren't kisses, though, and she hugged back and then quickly freed herself, searched his face. Because if there was even a hint of pity for her circumstances...

But all she could read in Linc's expression was bemusement, before he blinked and blinked again.

What had happened to her emotions just now?

They'd kissed, and that had been wonderful and amazing for her, but she needed to find some reality here. Linc's bemused expression might be for a hundred reasons. Hopefully, not because he knew she'd reacted as though her whole world had tilted on its axis when they kissed!

Pride surfaced as she confronted that absolutely untenable possibility. It was Valentine's Day. He'd kissed her. It could easily have been nothing more than a spontaneous act of the moment. Indeed, he could be regretting it even now, because of their business relationship. Remember? What would happen to that now?

It would be reinstated immediately—that was what! And for the sake of her pride Cecilia wanted to be the one to initiate that.

'I—I believe I'll do as you've suggested and head home. There'll be work again, bright and early in the morning, and it's been a long and busy day.'

Maybe Linc would put their kiss—or at least any vulnerability he might have detected in her as a result of it—down to the physical drain of the day.

She didn't wait to find out. Instead, Cecilia turned quickly and left him there to lock up, to secure everything.

'Goodnight.'

For the second time Cecilia abandoned her duty because her heart was in the way.

Not her heart! Her emotions. There was a difference—a really big difference. She had been overwhelmed by the power of the day and her exhaustion and missing her sister.

Oh, yes? And somehow that had made her trip and fall onto Linc's lips and kiss him and feel things she had never felt before? Even now she wanted to turn around, to go back, to extend her time in his company. Because...

Because of hope that shouldn't exist and that needed to be extinguished *now*—before it was allowed to grow any further. How could she feel this way? Be so drawn to him and in some part of herself so willing to leap in and believe he had some kind of emotional investment in her when no evidence whatsoever existed to prove that?

Linc wasn't offering her anything! One stolen kiss that might have happened without forethought or reason did not add up to...*anything.*

He was probably thinking already that it shouldn't have happened. And Cecilia would think exactly the same—just as soon as she could get her emotions unjumbled and back into some kind of reasoning, sensible order.

Maybe she and her sister were doomed to pick out the wrong men in their lives. Well, at least in Cecilia's case Linc would walk away from this moment, and it would fade to oblivion and be forgotten.

The same way Cecilia had 'forgotten' a six-year-old crush?

Fine. *He* would bury it and forget it. She might take a little longer to get to that point, but in the end she would.

She would!

CHAPTER FIVE

'YOU'RE LOOKING AT a classic nineteen-forties pram, luv.' The man selling the item turned the frame this way and that so Cecilia could get a better view of it. 'A bit of paint and you've got yourself—'

'A refurbished carcass missing all its interior parts?' Cecilia softened her words with a smile. 'I *do* concede that the frame is still in decent order. There's not too much rust.'

She named her final offer.

'It's that or no sale, I'm afraid. I have my buying limits, just as you have your selling ones.'

Cecilia was at a used-items fair in an outer suburb of Sydney. Hundreds of sellers had taken stalls both inside the pavilion and outdoors on the grassed area, and there were plenty of browsers and buyers there to enjoy the day.

She was doing her best to focus on her surroundings, but she was struggling. All she could think about was those moments with Linc at the nursery. What was *he* thinking? Had he thought about it at all? Or forgotten it the moment it happened?

Why had it happened, in any case? Had it been a moment of forgetfulness on his part? Had he seen the rose petal in her hair and that had led to an automatic response that might have happened anywhere, with any person? Maybe he'd intended a quick brush of lips or something and she'd prolonged that?

No. They'd both been equally involved. Hadn't they…?

This was what happened when a girl spent too much time revisiting a few special moments. She lost any shred of objectivity she might have had.

'All right, then.' The seller gave a brief nod. A twinkle of approval for her bargaining prowess flitted through his eyes. 'You can have it for that.'

'Thank you.' Cecilia finalised the transaction and told herself to draw a line under her thoughts about that kiss with Linc at the same time.

She had just handed over the money and turned to begin the task of taking the pram frame away when a deep voice spoke.

'I thought I saw a familiar face. Grabbing more items for refurbishment?'

It was Linc. A rush of warmth flooded into her cheeks. Oh, she hoped he wouldn't be able to see that in the dim lighting!

'Linc! I was just think—'

She had just been remembering a kiss that had left her confused and fighting herself, and now Linc was right here. She needed to step past that memory and not embarrass herself or let him see in any way how much those moments had affected her.

'How—how are you? What are you doing here?'

He'd seemed to materialise beside her as though from thin air. In fact, the air *did* seem thin around Cecilia in that moment. She could barely breathe.

Linc, in casual Saturday gear, was—well, he was *Linc.* The man she had kissed with such shattering impact on her equilibrium. And then she'd left him and told herself to forget all about it. But she hadn't managed very well. She hadn't managed at all.

Had it affected Linc in that way or not at all? And what was he doing here right now? *Oh, my.* What if he wanted to talk about it? To make sure she understood it had been a momentary slip in good judgment on his part or something?

Yet there'd been that bemusement in him, so maybe he had been affected by it, too?

And he couldn't have known he'd find her here today.

'I plan to fill the pram with snapdragons and baby's breath and mint.' She prattled the words with a breathless edge.

Get a grip, Cecilia!

She forced herself to slow down and to ask as casually as possible, 'What's brought you to the fair?'

Unfortunately, as she asked the question she allowed herself to *really* look at him. He looked amazing, in a polo shirt that emphasised the breadth of his shoulders and faded jeans.

He'd kissed her, and she'd seen stars and flowers and all manner of romantic things.

Well, wasn't she better off admitting that to herself? At least then she could start fighting the foolish feelings.

'My sisters-in-law plan regular outings for the family.'

His gaze roved her face as he spoke. And in that

moment of examination Cecilia was certain that the
memory of their kiss was in his eyes.

'Do—do they?'

'Yes.' He took a half step closer to her. 'They
wanted to visit the fair because it has a number of
vintage train sets and other vintage toys listed, and
Fiona and Jayne know that Brent is mad about those.
They…ah…they already have a restorer lined up to
work on anything we find today.'

*Oh, Linc. What's happening here? Do you feel
this?*

Cecilia realised in that moment that the hurt of
Hugh was over. It had given way to more immediate things.

The thought brought panic with it. Was she allowing those barriers to disappear because of Linc?
Surely that would do nothing more than open her up
to far greater hurt?

'It's sweet that Fiona and Jayne are doing that for
your brother.' And Linc was sweet too—for partici-
pating, for caring about his family.

There goes one corner of a barrier.

Fine. So maybe Cecilia *was* changed as a result of
their kiss. She would just have to make sure it didn't
show in any way that Linc could discern.

'Have you found anything?'

*Enlightenment? A desire for us to be together or
to find out more about these shared feelings that are
so amazing to me?*

And that probably didn't even exist for him!

'I've got a few items.' He pointed to the bag in
his hand and gave a short laugh, but his gaze still
searched hers.

Oh, how she wished she could simply read his thoughts.

'The girls went off together when we arrived, and Brent and Alex and I decided to split up and buy everything any of us came across and sort it out later. I'm not sure whether I've got junk or buried treasure, but at least I haven't come up empty-handed.'

Cecilia laughed. She just couldn't help it. This was a different side of Linc—a family-activities side— and it was adorable.

He smiled, and his gaze seemed to soften as he did so. That softening reminded her of when he'd kissed her.

So now she thought he was adorable, and she couldn't forget their kiss.

Bye-bye second corner of a barrier.

Don't you dare hope, Cecilia.

It was only as she warned herself against hope that Cecilia realised just how much she had allowed it to rise, despite all her warnings to herself.

Yet Linc was here, and she was here. Why couldn't she enjoy a chance encounter without getting bogged down in all kinds of worries and concerns and thoughts about who felt what? Linc wasn't making reference to their kiss, so why should she let it stop her from enjoying seeing him in this simple, everyday sort of way?

There. You see?

This didn't have to be a problem. She had let her thoughts run away with her, but she realised that now and would be able to bring them back into line. She and Linc had shared a kiss—it was over. He didn't seem to be about to mention it. She didn't have to, either. They could just act as though it had never happened.

The completely illogical nature of this decision-making process she simply ignored.

'What about you?' He glanced at the pram frame. 'Are you still looking around, or did you come just for that?'

'I've been here all morning, and I've got more searching to do.' She gestured towards the exit. 'But for now I need to get this pram back to my car and do something about lunch.'

That was fairly normal, wasn't it? She drew a deep breath and caught the scent of his aftershave…not blunted this time from a day's wear, as it had been when they—

'It's later than I thought.' He glanced at his watch. 'I must have got caught up in my browsing. Let me help you.'

As though he dealt with nineteen-forties baby carriages on a daily basis, he lifted the pram frame.

'Would you like to lead the way?'

Yes. Yes, I would. I'd like to lead you all the way to revisiting that kiss to see if I made up my reactions or if they happen again.

No sooner had the recalcitrant thought passed through her mind than Linc shifted his grip on the pram frame. The muscles in his arms flexed.

Had it just got really warm in there?

Not helpful, Cecilia.

'My car is beside the park.'

They left the building, crossed the road and Cecilia led the way to her car, where it stood at the edge of a public park. The vehicle was an old model, red because she hadn't been able to help herself and most importantly a hatchback, with seats that would lie down to make more storage space. She still felt completely flustered.

Linc tucked the elderly pram into her car. As he did so, he glanced at the items she'd bought earlier in the day. 'That's a nice load of junk—I mean *refurbishing items* you've got there.'

'Thanks.' She laughed and pointed to his bag. 'That looks quite bulky, and by the sounds of it you got quite involved in your shopping if you lost track of time. It seems I'm not the only one who has been engrossed in collecting junk—I mean *vintage items* today.'

Seeing shared amusement crinkle the lines around his eyes while his lips kicked up made her smile even more. She tried not to acknowledge that it also made her breathless.

Cecilia pressed the lock to her car and turned her back on it. 'Buying used items is a lot of fun. Maybe you'll want to keep doing it now that you've started?'

'Perhaps I will.' He gestured towards the park. 'My family are gathering for a picnic lunch. Join us. You said you were due for a break, and you can lend your expert opinion on the vintage items we've found.'

The invitation was casual, and yet her heart leapt stupidly and so easily.

Cecilia warned herself to thank him and say no. 'I guess I could take a look—but only if you're sure I wouldn't be imposing.'

'You won't be. They'll love it.' He started moving into the park, clearly expecting her to keep pace with him.

Cecilia did.

Fine. So she'd accepted his invitation? That didn't have to mean anything in particular. Lunch with his family didn't have to be a big deal unless she thought of it in that way. She'd obviously overthought the kiss they had shared, but if Linc could go on acting as though it hadn't happened, then so could she.

They made their way down a beautiful tree-lined avenue, past plane trees and palm trees and boab trees and a children's playground, and strolled up the curved path that skirted a classic fountain. Two soft grey pigeons rested right at the top, their heads close together.

Cecilia's glance remained fixed on them for too long, and she almost lost her footing on an uneven segment of the path.

'Careful.' Linc tucked her hand through his arm as though it were the most natural thing to do. 'It's tranquil here, isn't it?' He turned his head and glanced into her eyes.

'Yes.' She returned his glance before she looked away again. 'There's a sense of peace.'

They walked on in silence until finally she looked ahead and there, seated on a massive picnic blanket beneath the shade of a eucalypt tree, were Linc's family members. Two men. Two women. Each familiar to her.

She'd met them all before, at various times, but never in this kind of idyllic setting. Never while arm in arm with Linc and trying so hard not to make too much of that.

Cecilia dropped her hold of Linc's arm. 'Maybe I shouldn't—'

She thought he murmured, 'Maybe I shouldn't, either…' before he cleared his throat and said, 'I think it might be too late. They've seen you.' He gave his family a wave that on the surface at least appeared casual.

Cecilia forced her attention to the group. She glanced at the scattered bags the family had accumulated, particularly the pile beside Linc's sisters-in-law. 'It will be fun to look at the vintage items.'

'I thought you'd like doing that.' He gave a nod of his head. 'And I can guarantee the food will be amazing and there'll be plenty of it. Our family's housekeeper, Rosa, is an excellent cook.'

His family called greetings and, in the middle of it all, Cecilia found herself swept up into the heart of this gathering where she might have felt like an intruder and yet they made her so welcome that she simply couldn't.

Cecilia wanted to stay on her guard, but instead she relaxed as the family made her welcome. It *was* wonderful to be here, and if Linc's presence at her side contributed to that more than it should—well, she would simply have to worry about that later. She had no answers right now, anyway!

'Isn't it nice to enjoy the sounds of nature and this feeling of open space?' Brent's wife, Fiona, asked the question of the group. She glanced around. 'What a *great* way to relax.'

They all did exactly that. Cecilia examined the vintage train sets and toys they'd found and felt all of them had potential. 'I'm sure that some attention from a restorer would bring them right back to life.'

'That's what I thought.' Fiona returned a set of carriages to their faded box.

Conversation flowed across a range of topics after that and ended up rather randomly in a discussion about pet adoption before Cecilia began to notice the passage of time.

Linc had repeatedly drawn her into the conversation, as though he truly valued her thoughts and opinions. Somehow that made her feel safe.

Great.

That was all she needed—to start feeling *safe* around him. Self-delusion alert! She found the man attractive and interesting, but he was the owner of the business she managed—a millionaire, totally out of her reach. Did she even need to go on? What was safe about any of that?

Yes, but he'd also kissed her.

I don't believe he's not interested, said one side of her thoughts.

She pushed that side down, with the other side called *common sense*, and said in a bright tone as she forced her gaze around the group to encompass everyone there, 'This picnic food is delicious.'

'It is, isn't it?' Alex's wife, Jayne, encouraged Cecilia to take another lettuce cup, deliciously filled with seafood and a spicy dressing.

'It's nice to see you outside of a working environment, Cecilia,' Fiona said. 'We're so glad you could join us.'

'I was certainly surprised to see Linc when we bumped into each other at the fair.' Cecilia glanced at the man in question, where he half reclined in a very unmillionaire-like sprawl beside her.

How could one person look so alluring just by existing?

As she was about to turn her glance away again, Linc's mouth lifted at the corners. Just that and Cecilia's heart lifted right along with the turn of his lips.

She might have made her excuses and left then, but instead she became embroiled in a conversation about her refurbishing. Initially, it was with the whole group, but one by one they dropped out of the conversation to talk among themselves until it was only Linc and Cecilia left discussing the topic and she lost herself completely in it.

'If you outsourced the refurbishment work, that aspect of the nursery might increase its financial viability.' Linc made the statement laconically.

'At the moment it wouldn't,' Cecilia hedged, not really wanting to explain just why that would be the case.

'You're doing some of the work at home, aren't you?' Linc shook his head. 'I might have guessed you wouldn't stop at simply buying items on your own unpaid time.'

'It's a manager's privilege to donate time to the business.' She jumped in quickly to justify this. 'Besides, it's soothing work. I benefit from it as much as I give to it.'

'As much as I want to, I can't really argue with that.' His expression sobered as he went on. 'But I *can* encourage you not to let the work be a burden to you.'

'I enjoy it too much for that to happen.' Cecilia pursed her lips. 'You could be right about the outsourcing, though. Even if one of the lower paid staff took care of some of the basic work.'

'I was only teasing you.' Linc's gaze followed the movement of her lips. 'It's profitable enough as it

stands now, and I'm sure part of the charm for customers is your ability to sell the items on as the person
who breathed life back into them in the first place.'

'That does help.'

She realised then how close they were to each
other, that at some point each of them had leaned towards the other, and her heartbeat skipped. Her breath
caught in her throat. She had the sense that maybe he
wasn't as impervious as he was making out, and it
made her want to test that theory.

But they were here with all his family. This was not
the time for her to indulge in a state of superaware-
ness of Linc yet again.

She glanced guiltily around them, to discover that
she and Linc were now alone!

'Did we cause them all to leave with our—?'

'Our long-winded work-related discussion?' A
spark of devilment danced in his eyes, and this time
he *didn't* bank it down or try to stop her from seeing
his thoughts. 'Trust me, they're all just as bad—and,
no, we didn't drive them off.'

Cecilia fell into those eyes then and there. She simply softened to Linc and that was that.

Something had got into her that she couldn't seem
to control. It felt rather too much like anticipation,
happiness or maybe even hope.

'I find our discussions very enjoyable.' His words
seemed to emerge in a very deep tone.

Before Cecilia could fully register the pleasure in
his voice, he went on. 'My family have wandered off
to try to find an ice cream parlour somewhere, and
then head for their homes. There was some sign lan-

guage about all that just before they went, but you had your back turned at the time.'

'Going on about my refurbishing without noticing anything around me.'

She still felt a little mortified, but more than that she felt their shared consciousness of each other. She had to be sensing *that* correctly, surely?

'I should get back to the fair, too.' She forced herself to put more distance between them on the blanket and began to gather together the remnants of the family meal. 'Please thank the others for including me when you see them again.'

A part of her wished she hadn't made that belated decision towards self-preservation, but she had courted enough danger around Linc for one day. She didn't know how he felt, and until she could understand her own emotions better, she should keep her distance. The exact opposite of what she'd done today up until now.

Linc watched Cecilia gather plates and napkins and replace them tidily into the wicker picnic basket. With each movement she seemed to gather her barriers more closely about her.

Conversely, Linc's seemed to be slipping further away from him. Even as he watched her, he noted that she had beautiful hands, with slender fingers that were stronger than they looked—somewhat like Cecilia herself.

He'd gained great pleasure in drawing her out today. Knowing that she'd relaxed enough to forget her surroundings pleased him, too.

In all of it he'd told himself he *wasn't* thinking about their shared kiss, that his thoughts *hadn't* turned again and again to those moments and the emotions they had made him feel. Tenderness for her, and interest, a strong desire to know more of her—who she was and what made her tick and everything about her.

Those reactions didn't fall under the category of passing interest. He shouldn't have allowed any interest at all.

In truth, he shouldn't have invited her to this lunch. He'd told himself it would be a way to get them back on to a comfortable footing with each other, to leave that Valentine's Day kiss behind them, but that had been quite delusional—for him, at least.

He wanted even more to kiss her again.

Great going, MacKay.

And then, as though he had no control whatsoever over his own behaviour, he opened his mouth and added to the temptation.

'I'd hoped you might let me tag along this afternoon while you look over the rest of the stalls. There may be more train sets that I can pick up.'

Linc loved his brother. He totally did. And he'd cheerfully continue to buy Brent train sets if Brent continued to enjoy collecting them.

But why would Linc stay all day here, browsing for them, when the rest of the family had already left?

'You'd be more than welcome to join me.' Cecilia said it and bit her lip, but her eyes were luminous.

Immediately, Linc felt ridiculously pleased by that fact.

Fine. So he'd extended the time they would spend in each other's company today. So what?

He did what any good man would do in such circumstances, when he couldn't figure out which way was up or down in his life since a kiss had completely altered his perspective.

He pretended not to notice any of it.

The afternoon proved wonderful for Cecilia. She and Linc wandered the remaining stalls. Linc very quickly worked out the kinds of items that attracted her eye and pointed out several things to her that she would have otherwise missed. In turn she found two more vintage train sets that he purchased for his brother.

They laughed and made silly comments, and Cecilia remained constantly aware of him. Each time they bumped shoulders or had their heads close together over some item, her breath would catch.

Yet still she told herself that this was okay, that things were under control. That her attraction to him and interest in him *weren't* running full steam ahead.

Right or wrong, Cecilia felt happy for the first time in a long, long while, and she let herself relax fully into the feeling.

Maybe that was why at the end of the day, as they stowed the final item into her car and Linc turned to her, she remembered her sister in a sudden guilty rush and words poured out before she could stop them.

'I've had such fun today I forgot about Stacey completely.' Her words were low, almost inaudible and filled with guilt.

How *could* she have forgotten her sister so thoroughly? Especially now, when she should be waiting every moment for the call that would let her know when she could go to visit her?

Linc heard Cecilia's confession and she didn't need to say anything else, because those few words showed it all. The deep love, and the guilt that she had lived her own life for a few hours while her sister was shut away, only half living hers.

But there was a difference between a woman forgetting her sister for a few brief hours, when she couldn't do anything further to help her than she already was, and a man who'd completely neglected his brother's welfare for weeks at a stretch when he'd been charged with looking out for that brother.

While Linc acknowledged that he couldn't change his own past, he could offer comfort to Cecilia now. He opened his arms and pulled Cecilia inside them. 'It's okay. You haven't done anything wrong.'

His lips were in her hair, and for a brief moment her arms stole about his middle before she drew back. 'Thank you.'

Again, he watched her put herself back together, shore herself up and square her shoulders.

A feeling of pride in her welled. It may not be his place to feel it, but he did.

'Linc…'

In her beautiful eyes, and on her face, her appreciation for these moments showed. She seemed to be struggling to find words.

Linc struggled, too—against wanting to draw her close again. He knew he had to fight this awareness of her, that he should have fought it and won before they'd shared that Valentine's Day kiss.

Today he hadn't even controlled his urge to gain as much time with her as possible once their paths had crossed. In no reality could he justify that, when he knew there could be no future in pursuing that interest.

Linc needed to get his own boundaries back in place. That meant sticking to their working relationship. He shouldn't ever have allowed himself to waver from it.

'If there's anything I can do in terms of workload or freeing up your time to help with the situation with your sister, please tell me.'

Cecilia heard Linc's words and tried not to let them hurt her feelings. They came from the perspective of a business owner to one of his managers. She and Linc *were* those things, but even so…

She forced her chin up.

'Thank you. If there is anything I need in that respect I will let you know.' She gestured to her car. 'I must be going. It's been a nice day. I'll see you at work tomorrow.'

She couldn't be any more businesslike than that.

Cecilia congratulated herself all the way home. And if she also felt miserable and confused and unhappy in the middle of that congratulating, she buried those feelings in a flurry of repurposing work from the moment she stepped inside her front door.

It was good that she'd spent the day with Linc, because now she really did know that somehow she had to stop her thoughts and, yes, some of her feelings from running away with her any further when it came to her millionaire boss.

CHAPTER SIX

'HELLO, CECILIA? I'm just calling to seek your response to our invitation to attend the opening gala this evening.'

The words came from the president of the Silver Bells flower show organising committee.

'We don't seem to have heard anything back from you.'

The woman had called Cecilia at the plant-nursery office, and now Cecilia frowned with complete mystification as she registered the request. 'I'm sorry. I haven't received any invitation for the gala opening. I assumed it was for VIPs and organisers only when nothing came through.'

Cecilia *had* wondered but had put the thought from her mind as time had passed and the gala night had drawn nearer and still no invitation had been received.

'Oh, dear. I suspected that might be the case.' The woman's disappointment rang in her words. 'The invitation was to you and the business's owner. I'm afraid we outsourced the sending of our official invitations and a number of them appear to have been overlooked. That's a process that will definitely be changed for next year, but in the meantime we really *did* want to see you and Linc MacKay there tonight.'

'At such short notice I'm not sure—'

'It's *so* important to us, my dear.' The president sounded determined.

Well, the committee hadn't got such an amazing event into its inaugural year by hanging back, Cecilia supposed.

Cunningly, the woman went on. 'The masked ball will be one of our premiere events this year, and as its hosts we'd like to honour you. Surely there's a chance you could both make it?'

'I'll be delighted to be there.'

Cecilia would. This was an opportunity for her to promote the nursery and perhaps to gain some useful insights into the hopes the committee held for the rest of the month-long event.

Would Linc want to attend, though?

Cecilia's glance lifted and sought him out, where he sat at the other desk. As she glanced his way, Linc straightened from his computer, stretched his arms over his head and gave his shoulders a good roll. His head was turned, his gaze focused out of the window, so he wouldn't be aware of her eyes on him.

She was taking in the strong lines of his upper torso before she realised what she was doing.

'I...um...let me check and I'll get back to you. What exactly are the details?'

She scribbled down the return phone number, the start time, all the other information she needed, ended the call and turned to Linc, who was now working at his computer again.

'Linc?'

He looked up. 'Mmm?'

'An invitation that should have gone out asking both of us to attend the opening gala for the Silver Bells flower show was somehow overlooked. That was the president of the organising committee on the phone just now.'

A ridiculous flutter started up in her tummy as she went on.

'They are hoping we can both be there. There's just one problem. It's tonight.'

Cecilia refused to dwell on the prospect of spending an evening in Linc's company, if indeed he decided to attend. This was work related. He would either go or not go, depending on his level of interest and his schedule, and Cecilia wouldn't care one way or another. She had her feelings about Linc completely under control now.

Maybe he had a date with some beautiful woman tonight, anyway.

Worse, maybe he would bring one as his date to the gala!

Cecilia shouldn't care but, oh, she did. She cared about that possibility far too much. Suddenly, she wasn't at all certain that she *did* want Linc there.

'It's short notice. I understand if you have other plans.'

'There's nothing on my schedule that can't be changed.' His gaze showed only businesslike interest. 'If it will be helpful to your cause then I'm happy to make an appearance with you.'

With her.

Okay, so that was good.

In a purely business way.

Right.

So it was agreed that they would attend the event together. As colleagues.

Which was how it came about that just hours later Cecilia stood waiting inside her modest cottage home for Linc to arrive and collect her.

She didn't feel businesslike at all, no matter how much she tried to talk herself into feeling that way.

She wore a rose-pink evening gown with a soft cowl neck and fitted bodice. The gown fell from a high waist in gentle folds. Pearl drop earrings and her hair piled high on her head completed the look, and she had classic white high heels on her feet. Maybe the evening clothes were the problem...causing the flutter of excitement in her tummy right now.

Cecilia glanced again in her hall mirror and couldn't help but note that the person looking back was a far cry from the one who went off to work in casual clothes and sturdy boots most days.

What would Linc make of the transformation?

Not that she cared one way or another.

Indeed, she'd spent hours fussing over her make-up and hair just to please herself.

Outside, a car door closed. Inside her small home, Cecilia held her breath.

Moments later footsteps sounded on the short pathway to her front door.

Breathe, Cecilia.

Somehow the hopes and expectations for this evening's outing had got into her blood before the evening itself had even begun. The lift of anticipation only increased as the doorbell chimed.

She collected her purse, made the short journey to the door and pulled it open.

'Hi, Linc. Thanks for stopping by to collect me.'

She got the words out before she looked at him properly. It was just as well, because when she did, she couldn't drag her gaze away again.

He had on a sleek evening suit in a dark pinstripe grey, a crisp white shirt and a thin powder blue tie. Polished black dress shoes completed the outfit, and as he moved his arm slightly, she caught a glimpse of a gold cufflink.

Oh.

My.

Gosh.

Could *any* man look more handsome than Linc did tonight?

'Good evening, Cecilia.'

Linc spoke the words in slow response to Cecilia's greeting.

His first glimpse of her in a gown of deep pink shimmery fabric had stopped him in his tracks. All he could seem to see was bare sun-kissed shoulders, hair piled high on her head, showing off the lovely lines of her neck, and her beautiful face: eyes made up subtly to draw out their perfect blue depths, lips accented in a soft shimmery pink to match her dress.

'You look...' *Stunning. Gorgeous. Kissable.* 'Lovely.'

Even in saying that he felt like a master of understatement. What she looked was indescribably beautiful.

His intention to behave in a highly businesslike manner this evening seemed to have flown away as he stood there, his gaze caught in the bright blue depths of her eyes.

Linc tried to call that business mood back, but how could he as Cecilia's eyelashes swept down and she thanked him for the compliment?

When she glanced back up again, her gaze moved quickly over him and returned to meet his. A hint of pink tinged her cheeks.

'You look nice, too.'

The words were simple; the appreciation veiled at the backs of her eyes was complication bathed in blue.

'Shall we?'

He held out his hand for her to grasp before he managed a sensible thought. Led her to the car before he registered anything more than the subtle scent of her perfume—not floral this time, but something more complex and very alluring.

Only when he'd closed the door after helping her into the car did Linc take a moment to draw a breath and wonder what had just happened there.

This was not the first time he'd called for a beautiful woman to take her out somewhere. There *had* been women in his life. A number of them up until about a year ago, when it had all started to feel pointless and his dates had become further and further apart.

But seeing Cecilia tonight had literally taken his breath away. How could he deny his attraction?

Yet how could he do anything else?

In this moment he had no answers to any of it.

Linc strode to the driver's side of the car, opened the door and got in.

As Linc started the car, Cecilia stole another glance at him. Tonight he looked every bit the powerful and wealthy man about town. She might have always known it, but seeing him this way really brought it home to her that Linc was indeed a man who'd left his mark on life and would continue to do so.

She felt a little Cinderella-ish at the thought.

This is no fairytale, Cecilia.

In an effort to distract herself, she spoke. 'Did I tell you that tonight will start with a tour of the Gantry-Bell estate gardens?'

At least she'd said something, and furthermore something that didn't relate at all to how attractive she found Linc.

'Apparently, this will be the first time ever that the estate has been opened to the public. Given the name of the charity, and the fact that for a whole month people will be allowed to visit and tour the gardens, the committee must have cut a deal with the owners.'

They entered into a discussion about the flower show. Before she knew it, they'd arrived at the venue. Acres of beautiful gardens surrounded them on all sides, and in the midst of those gardens stood a mansion Cecilia would have expected to see in a fairytale.

'Oh, it's beautiful! Look at the ivy growing all the way up that south wall. There are turrets, too—just like on a castle,' she murmured, and then felt more than a little foolish for showing her awe so obviously.

'And a tower.' Linc stopped the car and handed the keys to a waiting valet, but he opened Cecilia's door himself and extended his hand to help her out. 'Isn't there a fairy story about a woman being trapped in a tower?'

'There's more than one story like that among the classic fairytales.'

In that moment *she* felt rather like a princess in a modern-day fairytale herself. A princess waiting to be swept away by a millionaire prince, perhaps?

Except Linc wasn't royalty, and nor was she and Cecilia was certainly not a damsel waiting to be swept away by a fantasy love in any way at all.

Would that be so bad, Cee?

She must not allow such thoughts even the tiniest space in her mind—and yet hadn't she already started to believe that she and Linc…

So unbelieve it right now—or you might find a pumpkin dropping out of the sky at midnight and giving you a concussion or bringing you a prince who could be a shoe salesman!

Yet they were here, and this *was* rather magical and Cecilia was tired of being practical all the time.

For the second time tonight, she placed her hand into Linc's outstretched one, and she *did* feel just a teensy bit regal as she alighted from his car.

At least until her gaze moved around them and she saw the other couples making their way to the front of the mansion. Couples dressed in similarly glamorous clothing and all looking completely at home in these surroundings.

Couples…

'Look…' She whispered the word to Linc. 'Up ahead. Is that that famous Australian gardening celebrity?'

The tall celebrity with his distinctive features turned and shared a laugh with the woman at his side. Cecilia knew for sure then.

'It *is*. I can remember watching his show when I was just a child.'

Cecilia felt even more out of her depth. A million-aire at her side, famous people all around her... Well, all right. She'd only seen one. But who knew who else might be there?

She on the other hand was just a girl who ran a plant nursery. A girl who happened to be at the side of that very same handsome millionaire just now.

'I can do this.'

She muttered the words beneath her breath, but Linc heard them, anyway.

'Don't tell me you're intimidated by your surround-ings, Cecilia?' He asked it with a teasing grin, as though he didn't have a care in the world.

Money would pave the way for that, she supposed.

Actually, Linc would pave the way for himself, whether he had money or not. Instinctively, Cecilia knew this.

So why should she be worried?

'I was a little awed by all this,' she admitted, 'but only for a moment.'

They made their way to the mansion's entrance, where they were met by the president, who'd called Cecilia earlier in the day.

'I'm so glad you're here.' The woman, a tall pow-erhouse in her late sixties, greeted Cecilia with an air kiss and clasped one of Linc's hands in both of hers. 'The committee are so happy you could both make it. We particularly want to catch up tonight.'

She gestured to a distinguished gentleman at her side.

'This is our host, Mr Gordon Gantry-Bell.'

'It's a pleasure to meet you.'

After a moment's small talk, their host gestured inside.

'Please make your way to the drawing room for light refreshments.'

As they strolled away, Cecilia turned her head to catch Linc's eye. 'I wonder what the committee want to talk to us about. Maybe it's just last-minute questions regarding the masked ball.'

The drawing room turned out to be a huge room, easily capable of holding three hundred people. A curved alcove made up of long sparkling windows looked out onto one aspect of the gardens. A grand piano filled the space in the alcove, and a man sat playing, his tall, thin frame concentrated utterly on producing the lilting melody.

Overhead, a long oval inlay graced the ceiling, and at its centre what must be a family crest in the form of an eagle was featured. Chandeliers hung at intervals along the ceiling. The room was stripped of furniture other than the piano and numerous oval tables spaced about. The pristine tablecloths bore the same eagle family-crest design, embossed into the cloth, while luxurious velvet-covered chairs surrounded each table.

'I really do feel as though I've stepped into another world.' Cecilia whispered the words even as she tried to ensure she had her most confident expression on as heads turned at their entrance into the room.

Immediately, another committee member separated herself from a small group of people near the entry, greeted them and introduced them to a number of other guests.

During a break in the flow of conversation, Cecilia leaned her head close to Linc's and murmured that she supposed they should do as others were doing and divide and conquer. After all, a room full of flower enthusiasts, sponsors and other interested parties allowed endless possibilities for networking. She shouldn't come across as though she wanted to cling to Linc's side.

'Don't even *think* about leaving me.' His low words sounded close to her ear, and her hand was lifted and tucked firmly into the crook of his elbow. 'The only conversation I have to offer about flowers is how to make money out of them.'

This was patently untrue, and Linc would be just fine on his own—Cecilia didn't doubt that for a moment. Still, if he wanted her company…well, that felt good. It shouldn't, but it did.

Minutes later the tour of the gardens was announced. Curtains were drawn back from a sweeping set of doors at the end of the room. These were thrown open with a flourish, revealing a vista of glorious colour and splendour so eye-catching on the other side that it was almost too much to take in.

'I've seen photos.' Cecilia almost whispered the words. She felt spellbound as they entered the gardens. 'But it's so much more when you're here. The perfect symmetry, the arches and blend of colours and shades, the different forms… I think these gardens may have taken some of their inspiration from the Butchart Gardens in Canada. This is so much more beautiful and complex than I realised when we first drove into the grounds.'

She understood now why the event would have

attracted celebrity interest—especially from a re-
nowned gardening identity.

'It is.' Linc glanced into her eyes, and his seemed
to shine with pleasure at her happiness. 'Brent and
Fiona would love to see all this. Their landscaping
and Fiona's artwork would both be inspired by it, I
suspect.'

'You *must* encourage them to come during the
month the gardens are open to the public, Linc.'

Cecilia herself felt inspired. Without even realis-
ing she was doing it, she clasped Linc's hand. His
fingers curled around hers and her heart expanded,
taking in the beauty and the pleasure of sharing it
with him.

They wandered at their own pace. Cecilia barely
noticed they had dropped behind the group at first,
but after a time she became intensely conscious of
the man at her side.

Would he think she had lagged behind deliberately? She hadn't.

But she couldn't deny that she wanted to be with
him right now and couldn't be sorry that the rest of
the group had moved ahead.

She forced herself to concentrate on this experience, and a thought occurred to her. 'The committee
have achieved something quite amazing in getting
these gardens opened up. They must be very determined.'

'And connected to the right people.' Linc added
this thought as they paused to admire an ancient sun-
dial.

Cecilia gave a contented sigh. 'This makes my efforts at Fleurmazing seem small-scale, doesn't it?'

'Not one bit. Don't downplay your success just because you're seeing something larger.' Linc held her gaze for a moment. 'Let it inspire you.'

'To even greater things?' She liked his philosophy.

'If you like.' Linc sounded relaxed.

Cecilia thought the gardens had worked their magic on him, too.

'My dears, we're about to make our way in. Will you join us at our dinner table?'

The question broke through Cecilia's reverie. The committee president had found them again. Indeed, it appeared the tour was over, because the entire group had dispersed and were making their way back to the welcome of the drawing room.

The president introduced another member of the committee. 'Do call us by our first names. I'm Susan, and this is Agneta. It would be such an honour to spend some quality time with you both.'

'Thank you,' Linc murmured.

'We'd be delighted,' Cecilia added and felt way too much like half of a couple.

She supposed she was—but they were a *business* couple!

They made their way to the table Susan indicated and took their seats. Shallow bowls filled with tea roses graced the centre and filled the air with their lovely scent.

At the urging of their hosts, Cecilia accepted a glass of white wine. The bottle looked French, and she suspected it would have cost her a week's salary. As she took a first sip she glanced at Linc.

His gaze was on her lips, and for just a moment in time their gazes met and held. Even her heart seemed to skip a beat, and then make up for it by beating fast.

'Madam…sir. Your entree.' A waiter discreetly placed fragrant plates before them.

'How long have you been in the plant-nursery business, Linc?' Agneta asked the question and gave a smile that was both coy and a little cheeky all at once. 'If you don't mind me asking, dear?'

Linc responded with the kind of smile and easy response that Cecilia would have expected if he'd been talking to an elderly aunty.

'I got into the business at nineteen after working two jobs and renovating houses until I had enough money to buy my first small nursery.'

Cecilia loved hearing this explanation. She'd never asked him these questions herself and took the opportunity to sit back and allow the older two women to grill him gently for all the information they wanted.

'And you, Cecilia? How long have you worked for Linc as a nursery manager?'

'Oh…' Guilty heat crept into her cheeks, because she knew she'd allowed the conversation to drift over her while she just enjoyed sitting beside Linc and hearing him share information about himself. 'It's been six years.'

They chatted easily with the committee members, getting to know others in the group as the evening wore on.

Cecilia was never unaware of Linc—whether he was talking to the committee member on his right or engaging in conversation with others around the table. She just couldn't seem to distance herself from a sharp consciousness of him.

She tried to focus her attention on the meal and on playing her part in the conversation. As the courses progressed from roasted fennel with blackberries to ocean trout and finally to a tangy lemon sorbet that was made with fruit from the lemon trees in the vast gardens, Cecilia felt tension building in the president and in some of the other committee members.

Tension was building within herself as well, but for different reasons. Sitting so close by Linc had her senses humming. Maybe it was the setting, the glamour or perhaps it was just that in other circumstances this might have been any girl's idea of a dream date. Whatever the reason, those two tensions—the one inside her and the one now being manifested by the committee—shortened her breath.

'No doubt you've both been wondering why we so specifically wanted to speak with you tonight.'

Susan's words brought Cecilia back to earth.

'We have a proposal that we feel will excite you. As you can see from tonight's gathering and our surroundings, the Silver Bells flower show will be prestigious from beginning to end. Now that we've inspected your maze and gained a clear insight into your plans for the masked ball itself, we know that yours will be a wonderful feature event, too.'

Here the woman paused and gave Cecilia an approving glance.

'Cecilia, we were pleased and impressed by your initiative when you approached us to make a masked ball at Fleurmazing one of our feature events this year. We believe it will complement the core activity of the flower show very nicely. Indeed—' here she glanced apologetically at Linc for a moment before turning back '—if the opportunity arose, we'd steal you to work exclusively on helping us with our arrangements for next year. A maze of the kind that you've produced at Fleurmazing, if undertaken here on these grounds, for example, could create a crowning glory for the event.'

Although it was said with a tongue-in-cheek smile, Cecilia didn't miss the keen look that accompanied it.

An opportunity to add to these beautiful gardens? To leave a creation of hers as a legacy to be enjoyed into the future?

'I'm stunned. Thank you. It's very kind of you to say such a thing.'

She glanced quickly at Linc and caught the shocked expression on his face before his brows came down and he quickly masked his thoughts.

'I'm certainly delighted to be holding the masked ball at the nursery this year.' Cecilia wasn't sure what else to say.

The group couldn't have asked her here simply to comment on her maze-making skills. There must be more.

'Regardless of any other possibilities, we'd like to offer Fleurmazing the chance to sign on now with us for future years.' The president drew a document from a satchel on the floor beside her chair. 'This outlines our offer in writing, but if I may elaborate now...?'

Her glance shifted to encompass both of them.

Linc was the one to respond. 'Please do.'

The president straightened in her chair. 'We'd like to bring our relationship with Fleurmazing onto a stronger footing for at least the next five years. We're in the throes of negotiating a contract with our hosts for the same time period, and we feel the two agreements would complement each other.'

She went on.

'Planning has already commenced for our second year of the flower show, of course. Imagine how great it would be to know at this stage that you'd be holding a masked ball for us again this time next year.'

'I'm flattered,' Cecilia said. 'It's wonderful that you'd like to continue the relationship into the future.' Her words were positive. She turned to Linc. 'I think you'd agree we should review the contract with a view to signing?'

'Definitely.'

Linc's response held just the right tone of business interest. Yet did he seem a little disconcerted, as well? Perhaps he hadn't liked it that the committee had all but offered Cecilia an alternative job right under his nose.

Cecilia smiled at the president, and then allowed that smile to encompass all those seated at the table. 'I would very much like to continue a working relationship with your committee, provided it can be done in a way that's workable for all concerned. If you'll allow us to examine the documentation, we will get back to you as quickly as we can.'

Later, as Linc drove her towards her home, she thought again about the committee's offer of an ongoing contract with Fleurmazing.

'That was an interesting way for the committee to handle their approach to us.' Cecilia made the observation quietly. 'I'm not complaining. It was a delightful night.'

As Cecilia spoke, she didn't seem to notice that she had slipped into using *us* rather than *the business* or even referring to herself as its manager. But Linc noticed.

He noticed it and he liked it. In fact, he had liked almost everything about this evening from the moment Cecilia had opened the door of her home and he'd seen how beautiful she looked.

To be so aware of her as a woman and to believe that she was equally aware of him had made it difficult to maintain distance in what had needed to be treated as business. Even in a setting of elegant glamour.

This shift in his interest in Cecilia should scare him. It *did* scare him.

'I guess the committee are looking to really cement their relationship with the Silver Bells owners.'

It also bothered Linc that the committee had all but offered Cecilia a job. He could see now that it had been naive of him, but he had never imagined Cecilia leaving his employ. The thought of it now made him uncomfortable.

Face it, Linc. The dividing line between a business and personal relationship when it comes to Cecilia is now irrevocably blurred. Just what do you plan to do about that?

'I don't blame the committee for wanting to consolidate. It's what I'd do in their shoes.' She nodded her agreement just as he drew the car to a halt outside her home.

Just so long as they don't take you from me in this 'consolidation'.

The thought came without Linc being able to

control it. Suddenly, the tie he'd been wearing all night felt constricting. With a tug he removed it and tossed it onto the console between them. 'At least that's gone.'

'Was it bothering you? You looked quite at home in all your finery.' Cecilia blurted the words, and then fell abruptly silent.

And everything changed, just like that.

No, it didn't change. Linc made himself acknowledge it fully. This need to pursue and build on what they had already shared, to take it further, to know Cecilia more wasn't a change. It was a truth.

'I—I should review that agreement tonight, before I go to— Before I turn in.' Cecilia said it as they alighted from the car. 'Did—did you want to come in, Linc, and look at it with me?'

'I'm happy to trust your judgment on it.'

They were some of the most difficult words he'd ever said. But they had reached her front door, and if he hadn't said those words, he'd have invited himself in and...

Silently, he held his hand out for her key. When she gave it to him, he opened her door and drew the contract from his breast pocket. He handed both to her together.

'You can tell me what you want to do tomorrow.'

Cecilia took her house key and the contract from Linc. Her fingers curled around both, and she felt the contract still warm from the heat of his body. It took will power for her not to hug that warmth to her.

'Thank you for attending the gala with me tonight.' It had been a night she would remember for a very long time. 'It was— I'm sure the committee must have been pleased that you were there. Good—goodnight.'

'Goodnight, Cecilia.' His words were deep.

She didn't know who moved, but somehow they were close, and he bent his head, and she lifted hers and all her good intentions, wobbly as they had been, disappeared.

Their lips met.

Cecilia's resolve, whatever it might have been in the first place, melted away. When his hands held her waist, her free arm wrapped around his neck and their kiss deepened naturally.

There simply was no hesitation—on Linc's part or on hers. Cecilia gave herself to this closeness and this man.

He tasted of lemon sorbet. She probably did, too. But more than that he tasted of Linc. Appealing and sensual and wonderful.

She said his name against his lips. 'Linc—'

'Cecilia.'

He spoke at the same time. His tone was low, and it let her know that he had been equally moved by their kiss.

One tiny shred of self-preservation surfaced within her. 'I have to go in—'

'I have to go—'

Again, he spoke at the same time, and she was glad then that she'd not asked him to come inside with her again, because he would have rejected her, and she'd been there before and it wasn't nice.

He stepped back and away from her, and she pushed her door open and stepped over the threshold.

'Goodnight, Linc. I'll see you at the nursery.'

She went inside and closed the door behind her, listened as Linc's steps faded away and his car door opened and closed. She heard the soft start of his car's engine.

He was gone.

CHAPTER SEVEN

'I'VE EARNED THIS TIME. Just fifteen minutes before I leave for the day.' Cecilia said it aloud, though there was no one there to hear her.

She was in the repurposing shed. She opened a can of paint, stirred it and carried it to an unfinished project.

Linc hadn't come in to the nursery today. He'd called to say he had to deal with the fallout from an overnight crash in the commodities market, and she'd been both relieved and disappointed by the news.

She'd prepared herself to see him, to acknowledge the kiss they'd shared last night and to say that it would be best if they focused on their professional relationship and didn't go there again. That was the sensible choice, and she needed to protect herself... to make sure she didn't get hurt again.

Couldn't you trust that this might be different from the disappointment you experienced with Hugh?

Actually, she was over Hugh. What she was really worried about was that she might allow herself to start to care deeply for Linc. It was her own developing feelings that scared her.

It would be for the best when Linc completed the

review and they could both just get on with their nor-mal lives again—as they had done before this started.

Good. Fantastic. That was exactly what she wanted, and she 100 per cent believed they could go back to exactly the way they'd been before.

'Sure. Why *wouldn't* we be able to do that?'

She slapped the paintbrush against the side of an old crate with a little too much vigour. Spots of paint spattered onto her shirt and shorts.

When her cell phone rang moments later, she an-swered without even looking at the caller ID.

It was her sister.

'I know this is short notice, but is there any way at all that you can come in to see me tomorrow?' Sta-cey asked the question in a rush of words. A hint of excitement crept through into her tone. 'I've got ap-proval for the visit, and I've made a booking for you in the morning group in the hope that you can make it. I understand if you can't come. I can book it for the following week. I just thought I'd ask.'

'Yes. I'll be there.' Cecilia didn't hesitate for a sec-ond. Emotion tightened her throat. A chance to see Stacey after so long… She would make it work! 'Oh, I can't wait to see you.'

'I'm so glad you're coming.' Stacey gave an au-dible sigh of relief.

They talked for a few minutes more before Stacey reluctantly ended the call.

Cecilia turned back to her painting, but her thoughts were filled with the upcoming visit to her sister.

She was deep in thought when she heard a footfall behind her. She swung around and there was Linc—and he looked so dear.

'Linc.' Here was her chance to talk about what had happened last night. 'You...ah...you gave me quite a start.'

'Is something wrong?' He stepped forward. Concern laced his voice. 'If it's about—?'

'No, no. Nothing's wrong at all.'

Instead of bringing up the matter of *them*, as she should have, Cecilia shied away from even mentioning it. Well, she had a major family matter on her mind right now!

'I just had a call from my sister, asking if I'd visit her tomorrow. I'll have to check that Jemmie can cover for me. I—I can't wait to go.'

The last sentence surprised her by being tougher to say than it should have been. Cecilia *did* want to see her sister. *So* much! It was just that it would challenge her emotions. The place itself and all that it represented... Her having to leave her sister there when she left... Having such distance from the reality of what Stacey was going through...

'That's great news.' His expression softened with happiness for her but also with a more sober emotion. 'Although I can't help feeling concerned about you going into that environment,' he said carefully. 'Even though I know you have no other choice if you want to see your sister.'

He had spoken the very concern that she felt deeply herself. But she couldn't speak of it, because it might make her sound selfish or unwilling.

Oh, Linc. You don't make it easier for me to stop caring for you when you show this caring side yourself.

The thought crept in, unannounced, and then it was

too late. She couldn't deny it. She *did* care for Linc. Her feelings had developed without her even wanting to allow it to happen.

What if those feelings continued to develop? What if she couldn't control them and…?

Why didn't you take the chance to say something just now, when it was right there in front of you? You should have drawn that firm line and given yourself the chance to get those emotions under control.

'It—the visit—will be fine.'

She would cope with how challenging it felt to pass through all those self-locking doors, the checkpoints, to feel hidden gazes upon her and not know who was looking or what they were thinking, because it meant a chance to see and be supportive to her sister.

Cecilia had visited Stacey just one time, and that had been such a disaster of a visit that she hadn't let herself think too much of how confrontational it had been in and of itself.

Well, Cecilia *had* to be fine.

'There are plenty of staff on duty in the visiting room. I'm sure if anything…worrying happened, they would know what to do.'

'Right. That's good.' He paused, and then couldn't seem to hold back his questions. 'What time is the… uh…the appointment? Fordham, isn't it? What amount of contact do you…ah…do you have with the other prisoners there when you visit?'

His questions about all the practical aspects of the visit were…well, they were adorable, actually.

Oh, Cecilia, you are in so much trouble with your feelings.

Perhaps, but it wasn't as though she loved him or anything. That would be beyond foolish.

She explained the details he had asked about. 'There will be other prisoners in the visiting room, where I'll see Stacey, but people keep very much to themselves. Fraternising with other groups is not allowed.'

Linc listened as Cecilia explained about her upcoming visit to her sister. With every fibre of his being he wanted to insist that Cecilia did not step foot into that place.

Surely there was some risk involved in being exposed to other prisoners and their visitors? What if someone decided to start a riot?

What if you let your mind run away with you a bit more, MacKay?

Yet at the same time he wanted Cecilia to go. This was her family, so of course she had to go. In the same circumstances—

In the same circumstances he had failed, in a way that had left his brother Alex paying the price. Linc had sworn an oath to himself that he would never let anything like that happen again.

He watched now as Cecilia turned and quickly closed up the paint can, tidied the area.

They'd kissed last night, and Linc had not been able to get those moments out of his mind. When he thought about her, his chest squeezed and he had an overwhelming need to...to be wherever she was— just so he could look up and she'd be there. What did *that* mean?

'I'd better call Jemmie and ask if she's happy to step in tomorrow and continue with the preparations for the masked ball.'

Cecilia's words broke through Linc's reverie.

She went on. 'I have an action list she can follow, but it's a really busy time.'

Linc welcomed this distraction from his thoughts, even though it brought him back to Cecilia's trip to visit her sister tomorrow. 'Everything is well in order, because you're such a good operator, so it will be fine. I'll come back to the office with you now.' He fell into step at her side. 'It's late to be starting, but I want to put some work in on the review.'

I stayed away from here all day but gave in and came looking for you, anyway.

He just hadn't anticipated that seeing her would fill him with warmth and something that felt rather like happiness.

'I hope that commodities crash didn't impact too badly on your businesses?' Cecilia made the statement to Linc and knew she should have done it earlier.

Did Linc want to work late like this because he couldn't wait for the review to be finished? Cecilia tried not to feel hurt at the thought.

He thanked her for her concern. 'It wasn't great, but these ups and downs happen.'

As they stepped inside the office, Cecilia brought up the flower-show committee's proposal. 'They're offering next year as a fairly solid proposition for Fleurmazing to host the masked ball again, with the proviso that the Silver Bells charity would still need to sign off on the overall plans for it all to go ahead.'

'That sounds reasonable.'

Linc took his seat at the second computer. He looked at home there now...as though he belonged.

The thought crept up on Cecilia and she frowned.

Linc didn't belong here. He belonged in his high-flying corporate world, running all his business interests and never giving her a thought.

She'd pushed for a review, and he'd rewarded her dedication by conducting it himself. Once it was done, that would be it.

But would it? Or had things changed for him, as well? Maybe he'd want to keep seeing her?

'The flower show committee want exclusive rights to the Fleurmazing masked ball for the next five years. I'm willing to give them that, but I'll want the contract updated first to spell out that Fleurmazing *can* conduct other celebrations and activities utilising the maze.'

'Well done.' His gaze met hers over the tops of their computer screens. 'It's clear you've considered this from all angles.'

She felt so proud in the face of his praise that it was difficult to keep a pleased smile from her face.

Tell him now that you want to be careful there's no repeat of what happened last night. Tell him. Because you can see for yourself that you're all but hanging off every word he speaks. You need to do something about your out-of-control and ever-developing feelings towards him before they truly get you into trouble.

'Thanks. I'd…um…I'd better make that call to Jemmie and then do my tidying up here for the night so I can get going.'

'Good idea. You'll need to get some rest tonight, too.'

Linc wanted to say more, to say that he enjoyed her company and didn't want it to end, but he stopped himself. An attraction that should have been easy for him to control seemed to be getting the better of him. Linc wasn't accustomed to that, and he didn't know how to address it.

Get his work here finished and remove himself from her life as much as possible, he supposed.

He ignored the knowledge that it wasn't only a physical awareness of her beauty and appeal that had him in its thrall and tried to focus on his review work.

Linc succeeded, somewhat, but his thoughts kept returning to Cecilia's upcoming visit to her sister at the correctional centre the following morning. To the kisses that he and Cecilia had shared. To this whole situation and how it was making him feel.

He needed to start working out just exactly *why* Cecilia was impacting on him the way she was and put a stop to it.

Yes, sure—he would work all that out and get it under control in no more than a blink of an eye and with a few minutes of careful thought and concentration.

He'd probably find the answer to world peace while he was at it…

CHAPTER EIGHT

'I'M READY. It's okay to leave early. There's nothing else I need to check or make sure about. It's time. I'm going to see Stacey.'

Cecilia said the words aloud as a means of stopping herself from fussing any longer, checking and rechecking that she was prepared for her visit to her sister.

It was 7:50 a.m. She had a lengthy drive to get to the facility, so leaving sooner rather than later made sense.

And if she was struggling to breathe through an onslaught of anxiety, if her heart was thumping—well, it was with hope and excitement, too. Stacey had realised she'd made mistakes, and she was choosing to set a better path for her life for the future. One that included her sister in it.

Cecilia pushed back the sudden surge of emotion—relief and hope for Stacey, and worry and pain for where her sister had landed herself already. She couldn't indulge such things right now.

She stepped outside, closed and locked the door behind her, and made her way along the short path.

Out on the street a man leaned against the back of

her car—a very familiar man, who removed his sunglasses and straightened as she approached.

Oh, how her emotions leapt in that moment of recognising him.

'Linc! What are you doing here?'

She didn't know what to think. In fact, her mind seemed reluctant to process more than how the sight of him made her heart ache a great deal less, and more, all at the same time.

'I know you won't have been expecting me.' His words were roughened, as though pushed past emotion. 'There might not be anything else I can do that'll take some of the strain off you, but I want to drive you there and back today. If that's okay with you?'

It wasn't pity. She knew that immediately. But had this come simply from an employer's sense of duty towards his employee?

She searched his face and saw the way his jaw clenched. As their glances locked and held, the deep steel grey of his eyes softened.

No. This wasn't about work. This was personal—a man wanting to help a woman he cared about. Cecilia was certain. That *had* to be what she was seeing!

Her emotions wanted to take hold of this and run with it. But she cautioned herself that any measure of affection that Linc now felt could be *any* measure. She did not need to set herself up to expect more and then be hurt.

So don't go hoping too much about Linc's feelings towards you. In fact, why are you even pondering that when your focus needs to be on your sister?

It was easy for Cecilia to use that thought to push aside any need to trust Linc beyond that. She didn't make any correlation to the impact of Hugh deserting her, and the blow that had given to her self-worth as a partner, but it was there in the back of her mind.

'Thank you, Linc, for coming here for this.'

His offer to drive her to the facility did mean a lot. She would thank him and say she would go on her own.

But Cecilia knew that she wouldn't do that. His company today, his willingness to be there for her... She simply couldn't turn her back on that, caution and past history or not.

'I would be grateful for your company, to tell the truth.'

As though to confirm her earlier hope about his feelings for her, he took an involuntary half step towards her and lifted one hand.

Oh, Cecilia, are you sure you want to believe that he really cares about you in an emotional sense?

Because that was what she was trying to do right now—to imbue Linc with a deep and personal caring feeling towards her when he could just as easily be feeling concern for a colleague he happened to have kissed a couple of times.

But sometimes people denied that they were emotionally entangled when in fact they really were, so could he be?

Was she saying that *she* was emotionally entangled in Linc?

No.

Maybe a little.

Can't you just accept his help today, just this once, because it will make the trip there and back easier for you, and not think about the rest of it? Focus on Stacey. That's more than enough to worry about.

'So if you really do have the time, Linc, I'd love the company.'

'I do, and I'm glad to hear it. I need—'

He cut himself off, but his shoulders eased.

Instead of finishing his previous thought, Linc simply said, 'Do you prefer that we go in your car or mine?'

'I'd rather it be my car. The parking area is underground, so you'll be able to wait there if you want, or you could come with me to the reception area and stay there while I—while I go in. You can't bring a cell phone with you, though, not even in the car.'

'That won't be a problem. My phone is in my car, and it can stay there until we get back.'

Linc took the driver's seat of Cecilia's hatchback car. He had to push the seat right back to fit his legs in comfortably. In truth, he'd deal with any amount of discomfort to ensure Cecilia didn't have to face this day on her own.

He'd known yesterday, when she'd first told him she was going to the correctional centre today, that he would want to go with her.

Linc hadn't understood the fierceness of that need at the time, and he had fought it because he hadn't known what she would make of it if he *did* ask to go with her. He had fought right up until he'd woken at five this morning, and then he had stopped fighting it.

He still didn't completely understand the strength of his feelings for Cecilia, but he could no longer go on pretending they didn't exist. Linc needed to know.

Somehow, yesterday, when Cecilia had told him she would be coming to visit her sister, something inside him had changed. He hadn't been able to let her face this on her own. That hadn't simply been about wanting to protect another person. If it had, he'd have been able to explain it away. He couldn't bear not to be a part of this with her. Linc needed this for himself.

All he could do right now was accept the need and be grateful she was allowing him to act on it—hope that a greater understanding of what was going on inside him would come.

'I'll give you the directions.'

She proceeded to do exactly that as they began their journey.

'Tell me about Stacey.'

I would love to know more about your family, your past, all the things that matter the most to you.

'What was your favourite thing to do together when you were little?'

He hoped, too, that talking would help take her mind off the more confrontational aspects of the day ahead.

Cecilia shared some memories from her childhood. Playing games with her sister…finishing each other's sentences.

'Our mother wasn't very loving towards us, but having each other helped. We look significantly alike even now, but we aren't identical, so we couldn't get away with switching places with each other. We used to daydream about it, though.'

Sharing those childhood memories now had brought a smile to Cecilia's strained features, but when she had first stepped out through her front door that morning, anxiety had radiated from her.

Linc felt it himself—on her behalf. He also felt the disappointment of knowing that she hadn't been surrounded by a loving family all her life. Every person deserved that, in his opinion. And now she had another hurdle to get over.

'I wish I could go in with you this morning.'

'Stacey would raise her eyebrows a bit if you did that!'

Cecilia managed the quip and even a laugh to go with it. Linc had done her a world of good by coming along this morning. Oh, how her heart had lifted when she'd seen him—but she couldn't tell him that!

'Unfortunately, you have to be booked in advance to visit, so it wouldn't be an option today, anyway.'

'And you'll want your sister all to yourself.' He said it in a matter-of-fact tone. 'I wouldn't expect anything else.'

They covered the rest of the trip speaking intermittently of matters of no importance. It helped her fight off the nerves until they drove into the underground parking area.

Rather than dwell on her unease at the upcoming visit, Cecilia got straight out of the car when Linc stopped it. He alighted, too, and she had to confess— silently, at least—that she was rather glad he would be with her for as long as possible before she went in.

After that it was identification, registration, the wait while names were called, until finally it was her turn and she got up. Linc quickly pulled her tight against his chest and released her again.

Cecilia made her way through all the security processing. She was electronically scanned and had to pass a drug-detecting dog's assessment. A band with a number on it was affixed around her wrist. The officers were professional, but she couldn't help a feeling of being just that number to them.

Did her sister feel that way? Of course she would.

An officer checked her wristband. 'You're at table twenty-three.' The woman pointed towards a separate building and gave some other instructions.

Cecilia drew a deep breath. 'Thanks.'

Once seated inside, Cecilia fixed her gaze on the inmates' entry point and waited. She wished Linc were there with her and was comforted to know he was waiting for her outside.

After what felt like hours but was probably only minutes, her sister stepped into the room.

'Stacey. Oh, I've missed you so much.'

Cecilia stood and hugged her sister and felt relief rush through her as Stacey hugged back just as hard. When they drew apart and took their seats, Cecilia looked carefully at her sister.

Stacey wore a dark green T-shirt and matching pants, with trainers on her feet. Around her neck was a chain with a tag on it. Had she lost weight? Or was it stress giving her that lean look?

Cecilia pasted a big smile on her face. 'I brought coins for the vending machine. Would you like something?'

'Maybe in a little bit.' Stacey's hands fidgeted together on the tabletop until she stopped herself.

'Would you rather just talk first, Stace?' Cecilia wanted to take her sister's hands but had to settle for hoping her love for her sister shone from her eyes.

'I made such a stupid mistake.' Stacey said the words quietly before looking up to meet Cecilia's gaze. 'Running around being an idiot with Joe and not getting out of the situation when I realised I'd got myself into something I didn't like and wanted nothing to do with. I wish I'd never met him. I'm not saying this is all his fault. I made the choice to be with him. But I don't want anything to do with him now. Not ever again!'

Cecilia drew a deep breath. 'I'm glad you've decided not to have any part of him now.'

Stacey glanced around them briefly, and then returned her gaze to Cecilia. When she spoke, it was in a quiet tone. 'He put me in a scary position—led me to believe that whole situation was very different to what it turned out to be. And when it all went wrong, he left me there to face the consequences while he disappeared.'

'It's not always easy to see what people truly are, Stacey.' Cecilia knew that from the time she'd spent with Hugh. 'Sometimes it's not until they let you down that you can see it. Anyway, I'm glad you've left him behind you. That's good.'

'It is.' Stacey gave a wan smile. 'And now I can find my way back from how I've messed up my life. I'm going to have to.'

Before Cecilia could respond, Stacey went on.

'I got in the habit of being rebellious years ago, because it helped me to feel better about the way Mum gave up on us.'

'That wasn't our fault. The problem was with *her*.' Cecilia had carried her own anger and hurt over it. To some degree she probably always would. 'It's up to us to choose how we let that influence us now.'

'I'm choosing to do what I can to get out of here on good terms and follow a better path once I do.'

They talked about Stacey's future then and about Cecilia's life too—the plant nursery and the upcoming masked ball, but not about Linc. The time disappeared so quickly. Before Cecilia knew, it they were being told that the visit was over and Cecilia had to leave.

Reluctantly, Cecilia got to her feet and hugged her sister goodbye. 'I love you so much, Stacey.'

'I love you too, Cee.' Stacey used her pet name for Cecilia, and for a moment her eyes shone with the sheen of tears before she resolutely blinked them back. 'I—I'll see you at your next visit, but I'll call you. I'll stay in contact now—that is, if you'd like—?'

'Yes!' Cecilia smiled past her own emotion, and then she was on her way back through all the checkpoints until she arrived in the waiting room.

She couldn't help but feel happier. She would come back and visit again soon. They could talk again. Stacey would call, so they could stay in contact. Cecilia felt as if a missing piece had finally been replaced back in her life.

Linc wasn't in the waiting room, and the clerk informed Cecilia that he'd been sent to wait in the car. 'We don't allow people to remain in the waiting room if they have no reason to be here.'

Cecilia was on the pathway outside, still some distance from the parking lot, with her thoughts on the future, when Stacey could live her life again outside of this place, when a man suddenly came up beside her.

He grabbed her wrist in a punishing grip and lowered his face close to her ear. It all happened so fast she wasn't sure what was going on.

'What did you say to your sister to turn her against me? What did you say to her in there just now? Tell me!'

Fear and adrenalin shot through Cecilia. Who *was* this? What was going on? Her head whipped around. She caught a glimpse of largeness, tallness, of a face tightened by anger and hair the colour of wheat, cropped close to the man's skull.

This had to be Joe. It couldn't be anyone else.

'Let me go.' Cecilia said it in a low tone as she tried to pull free.

His grip around her wrist tightened. 'I know where you live, Cecilia. I know lots about you.' His voice was harsh. 'Trust me, you don't want a visit from me. So stay away from Stacey. Stop putting ideas in her head about getting out early and anything else you might have in your mind. She's better off doing the full term. When she gets out that way, she's free. No one will be watching her, checking her every move. She can go back to supporting—' He broke off.

'She shouldn't have ended up in there in the first place.' Cecilia forgot to be afraid as protectiveness for her sister drove the words from her. 'What kind of man leaves a woman to pay for his crime?'

'I make my own rules—and you've just pushed me too far.'

He started to pull her forward, and Cecilia wasn't strong enough to hold back. Fear ripped through her as she stumbled and fell into him.

And then Linc was there, breathing hard. 'Get your hands off her!'

For a moment Cecilia didn't know if Joe would obey, but then he uttered a curse, let go of her and ran off. He leapt into a car at the end of the parking lot, and the car roared away.

'I'm driving.' Linc spoke the words as he pulled open the driver's side door of her car.

Cecilia hadn't even been aware of them making their way back there. Her ears were buzzing and she felt light headed.

Don't you dare hyperventilate or faint.

'What just happened?' Linc rapped out the question. 'What did that guy say to you before I got there?'

Cecilia climbed into the passenger seat and noted that her hands were shaking so much she had to try twice to fasten her seat belt.

'That was Joe—the man who was with my sister when she got caught committing a robbery. Stacey's told me that Joe was the mastermind, and I've no reason to doubt that. Aside from some teenage rebellion, my sister never did anything criminal before she became involved with that man. He's been sneaking messages in to her. But she's seen his true colours and wants nothing more to do with him, and he...he isn't happy about that.'

'Why would he be here this morning? He can't visit her. He'd be picked up as soon as they recognised who he was.' Leashed power echoed in each word Linc spoke as he drove the car through the parking lot. 'We have to report this to the police. There's a station not far from here. We'll go straight there.'

'Yes, I think we'd better.' Cecilia laced her fingers together tightly so their trembling wouldn't show. 'I don't know how he knew that I'd be visiting this morning, but I believe he was waiting specifically for me. He basically implied just then that he would harm me if I didn't stay out of Stacey's life.'

'Is that what your sister wants? For you to stay out of her life?'

'No!' Cecilia said it with vehemence. 'We may look at life differently at times, but we love each other. We...well, we really did mend our issues just now. I promised I'd keep coming to see her, and she promised she'll call me when she can.' Cecilia drew a deep breath.

'I'm glad to hear that.' His tone of voice underlined the truth of this before he went on, 'You could have been really harmed just now.'

'You could have been hurt too, Linc.' Her words were low as remorse began to fill her chest. 'I shouldn't have asked you to come with me today.'

'I asked if you'd let me. There's a difference. And this is not your fault.' Linc's jaw clamped into a tight line. 'If I hadn't got there when I did—'

'He would have dragged me into his car, and I dread to think what would have happened to me.' Cecilia suppressed a shudder. 'Thank you for being there and for acting so quickly to scare him off.'

They made their way to the police station, spoke to the police, looked at images, and found out in the process that Stacey's Joe was operating under an alias. He was wanted not only for the armed robbery in Australia, but for a string of other crimes in his home country of New Zealand—some of them very serious.

The police over there had been trying to catch him for two years.

'I don't think Stacey knows any of that.' Cecilia spoke as Linc drove towards her home after the interview with the police. They would meet officers there to ensure her house was safe.

Linc shook his head. 'The police said he can lay the charm on when he tries. He must have hidden a lot of the truth about himself from her.'

'He must have. It makes me scared for her, as well as for myself.' She pushed the words past a lump in her throat.

There was a long pause while Linc's hands maintained a death grip on the car's steering wheel. The street was quiet. Then he pulled over into a parking space, unclipped his seat belt and hers and pulled her into his arms.

The strength of Linc's hold let Cecilia know how concerned he had been for her safety.

Barriers Cecilia had tried to keep propped up fell away. Her arms tightened around him.

He didn't say a word. Neither did she. But, oh, it felt good to be held and to hold him.

'That situation ranked right up there with some of the worst moments I've experienced in my life.' The words were almost wrenched from Linc as he held Cecilia close. 'If he'd harmed you—'

He drew back, and his gaze searched her face, travelled over her. He lifted the wrist the man had gripped. Red marks showed on the delicate skin. Everything inside Linc cried out for justice, for the man who had done this to her to pay for it. In those few moments in time, he let his eyelashes sweep down, because he didn't want Cecilia to see his roiling emotions.

'There will be a bruise, but that's all.' Her words were soft, hushed almost and edged with a need for reassurance that she probably didn't realise was there.

Linc lifted her hand and pressed it against his chest, laying his own over it. His need to give to Cecilia won out over his memories and the guilt from the past. The emotions he felt, this need for connection, just couldn't feel wrong to him in this moment.

The knowledge sent a warning signal through him. But with so many other emotions churning, that signal quickly faded and disappeared. He gently kissed her, and then there was no thinking at all—just experiencing.

Cecilia's lips parted beneath Linc's as she gave herself to kissing him. Her lips softened, yielded to him and received from him at one and the same time. Her defences were down and she needed this.

They kissed softly and gently, exploring each other and healing the fear of those earlier moments.

And then a thought came to Cecilia.

She'd reconciled with her sister.

Surely that meant that anything could be possible.

She and Linc could be possible...

Once that last thought surfaced, there was no taking it back. It changed her. It infused her with hope. And while the common sense side of her warned that such hope was not wise, she couldn't heed it.

When they finally broke apart, Linc seemed to let her go reluctantly.

He sighed and restarted the car. 'We'd better get moving. Now, talk me through the layout of your home.' He cast a quick, apologetic glance her way. 'I'd like to know before we get there. I remember from this morning that there's no place in the front that a person could hide. I could see all of it while I was waiting for you. What about the sides and the back? Would it be easy to break in from any of those points?'

'I've never thought deeply about any vulnerabilities there in that way.' Cecilia forced herself to think about it now. She'd forgotten the threat of Joe during those moments in Linc's arms.

Oh, how easily she had forgotten.

'The back door is deadlocked, and all the windows have locks, but the house isn't alarmed. It backs onto a neighbouring property, but I guess that wouldn't really stop anyone. A person could also enter from the front yard and walk down the left side. The bathroom window is halfway down on that side.'

When they were several blocks away from her home, Linc spoke again. 'The police suggested you don't stay there for the time being. I'm holding you to your agreement to that advice.'

'I know I might not be safe.'

In a way she'd been waiting for this—and also dreading him bringing it up, because it forced her to think about the implications. The thought of being forced out of her home and looking over her shoulder until this situation could be resolved was hard to take.

'There's work, too. That will have to be managed so no one is placed in any danger. Oh, goodness! The masked ball. What am I going to do?'

'That isn't upon us yet, so let's worry about one thing at a time. We'll sort this out, Cecilia. I promise you.'

His calm words helped.

'For now I want you to wait in the locked car while I let the police in so they can check your place. Once I'm sure it's safe, you can gather some things together.

The police said they'll have a car there watching until further notice, in the hope that Joe *does* follow through and turn up.'

Linc stopped the car two doors down from her home.

She identified her front door key for him.

He reiterated that she was not to get out until he came back and gave the okay.

'How do I know you'll be safe?' The question burst from her at the last moment.

The smile he gave had an uncompromising edge to it. 'I'll be careful. You don't need to worry about my safety.'

She worried anyway, and it seemed he was gone for endless minutes before he returned to the car and told her he was satisfied she could safely enter her home.

Cecilia entered, retrieved her phone and started packing an overnight bag. It was reassuring to have Linc with her and to know that the police were watching from across the road in their unmarked car.

'Pack for several days.' Linc made the suggestion from the living room. It was the one place where he could see both her and the front and back doors. 'Since we don't know yet exactly what will be happening, I think that would be best.'

She packed. They left quickly.

Cecilia let herself think then about where she should go, and realised Linc seemed already to have a plan in his mind, if his confident driving gave any indication.

Rather belatedly, she asked, 'Where exactly are you taking me?'

CHAPTER NINE

'You've left your car at my house.'

Cecilia not only didn't know where Linc intended to take her—she didn't know what might happen to his vehicle if he left it outside her home.

'I made a couple of calls when I retrieved my phone out of it. Alex and Brent are on their way to collect my car.'

Linc's words were matter-of-fact, as though he called in his family to sort out other people's problems on a daily basis. As though he didn't find it strange at all to be helping Cecilia deal with this entire issue.

'The police will be watching, so I've let them know Alex and Brent will be doing that.'

'Okay. That's good to know.'

She couldn't deny that it was reassuring to have Linc's level-headed input just now. Was this what people experienced when they entered into a truly meaningful partnership? This alignment of emotion to the needs of each other?

Not that she and Linc had entered into such a thing.

She, however, *had* entered into believing it could be possible.

Not a smart way to start thinking, Cee.

Yet she couldn't undo the thoughts. They were a part of her now, and they did not want to be denied. She needed time to consider them, to think it through rationally and ask herself whether there really might be a chance and what that might entail.

Could she see Linc for a period of time, enjoy wherever it might lead them and then let it end with no regrets? Because wouldn't that be all Linc would offer?

'It's good of Alex and Brent to help.' She knew she was dodging her own question. 'Please thank them for me when you can.'

'Not needed, but I will.' He drew a deep breath before he spoke again. 'I want you to stay with me tonight, Cecilia.'

For a moment she felt as though he'd read right inside her mind just now, and her heart fluttered, but then she realised there must be a different motivation for his statement.

'It's good of you to want to keep me safe.'

If you'd asked me to stay for other reasons, I'd have agreed instantly.

Maybe it was just as well that he hadn't!

She cleared her throat. 'But I'd planned on going to a hotel.'

'I don't feel that would be safe enough.' His response was immediate and firm. He went on, 'We're heading for my place in the city. The building has excellent security. I realise I didn't ask you first. I should have. That scene back there left me more shaken than I care to admit, I guess, but I know I do need your agreement. I'll take you to a hotel if you insist, but please don't.'

Any problem she might have had over him not seeking her agreement first evaporated in the light of that final request.

Oh, Linc, you become more lov—likeable by the minute.

'I've only ever seen your warehouse building.'

That near slip-up in her thoughts shocked Cecilia so much she struggled to maintain an even tone of voice. It was one thing to contemplate seeing where a relationship might go with Linc in the short term, but to almost think the L-word about him was a whole other matter!

'I maintain both. The family all get together at the warehouse regularly. Rosa keeps everything ready for us.'

He shrugged his shoulders—a wealthy business-man with a busy lifestyle and the financial capacity to make that lifestyle as workable as possible for himself and for those around him.

'I guess that would make sense for someone in your position.'

She'd known he had other properties and that both brothers had moved out of the warehouse to other homes. But knowing she was about to enter another one of Linc's properties did remind her of the disparity in their circumstances.

Well, from Linc's perspective it would be the height of practicality to have a place in the city. If Cecilia wanted to think about anything, it should be how she was going to manage the rest of her commitments while this was all going on.

Yes, Cecilia. Maybe you should be thinking about

the actual circumstances that have brought about this temporary change in your place of residence.

And she should also be thinking about what she could do, if anything, to try and help get that man caught, so she could get back to her normal life and be totally sure Joe was out of Stacey's life for good.

'I appreciate your offer, and I'm grateful to accept the security measures that will go with it.' She forced her voice to remain as steady and even as his had been. 'I need to figure out how to manage things at work. I have to get back there. There's so much to be done, and I also need to make sure the staff are safe. What if this guy knows where I work, as well?'

'There are certainly measures that need to be taken, and the police don't have infinite resources.' He said it carefully, as though feeling his way.

When he went on, Cecilia understood why.

'I've asked Alex and Brent to arrange a security firm to provide around-the-clock surveillance at the plant nursery until further notice.'

Rather than contesting or questioning this, Cecilia simply expressed her gratitude.

'Thank you.' She would worry about what that would do to the business's bottom line later. For now the important thing was that everyone would be safe. 'That will help when I return there, as well.'

With a suppressed sigh she changed the subject.

'I need to make that phone call to the centre now. I know the police were going to alert the staff to what happened in the parking lot, but I need to put a request in for Stacey to call me. I haven't even had the chance to tell you that we had a genuinely wonderful reconciliation this morning.' Cecilia fell silent for a moment. 'I hope this happening won't undo that progress.'

'I'm glad you got that result with your sister, and I'm sure she will want to continue being closer to you.' Linc drew the car off the street, and his words rang with sincerity. 'We've arrived.'

'I didn't notice we'd come so far.'

They were on an affluent street in one of the city's most sought-after suburbs. A beautiful multistorey building loomed before them. It had secure underground parking. Other cars must also park there. Yet Cecilia saw only Linc's private parking area as they drove in.

At least by focusing on those details she could distract herself away from her softening emotions towards Linc.

Yes, Cecilia, but those emotions are still there. What are you going to do about that?

Fine. Maybe there *were* emotions. But it had been an emotional day. She didn't need to do anything about…anything.

So she stated the obvious instead. 'You're the owner of the whole building, aren't you?'

'Yes, it's one of my investment properties.' He said it without any particular inflection. 'Holding an apartment here works well for when I need to meet with my business broker or take care of other business without the trouble of going in to the office.'

Yet he and his brothers had created their own return-to-the-family oasis out at the warehouse building after the other two had moved out. Cecilia liked that concept, too. It spoke of a close-knit family who, while they went about their individual lives, still needed to reconnect on a regular basis.

That was what she'd had with her sister when they were younger, and now she believed she would have again. She *did* believe it and felt better for giving herself that reminder.

Minutes later they were safely ensconced in Linc's apartment on the top floor. The harbour views were magnificent, and the apartment was furnished in elegant yet comfortable style. A squashy black leather sofa and matching chairs dominated the lounge area. The kitchen shone in chrome, with a white marble workstation in the middle.

'This is—'

Opulent. And yet it was still Linc. A demonstration of his vast wealth, and yet it felt welcoming. Maybe that came from the clutter of kicked-off male shoes and boots inside the door, or the scatter of financial magazines tossed down beside one of the armchairs.

'It's a great place, Linc.'

Linc might wear jeans and work boots and look like a regular working man much of the time, but he *was* a millionaire—a self-made success story. This apartment certainly testified to that fact.

'I'm glad you like it.' He shifted her bag in his grip. He'd insisted on carrying it in for her from his car. 'There's a guest room through here.'

They passed a room that must be his, and an office, and came to the guest room. With her bag stowed inside the door, and Cecilia determinedly refusing to think about Linc's bedroom just an office space away, she followed him back into the living area.

'I don't know what to do.' She'd murmured the words before she realised she had spoken aloud.

About my feelings, about that threat, about anything at all right now!

'It will be okay, Cecilia.' Linc spoke the words from the open-plan kitchen.

He was boiling the kettle and had mugs, coffee granules and a teabag at the ready. Right there, in that chrome and marble masterpiece, Linc MacKay was preparing a fortifying cup of tea for her and making coffee for himself while he was at it.

Who was he, really? Which man was the real Linc? The one dressed in work boots and casual clothes who would drive a woman to a correctional facility first thing in the morning so she could see her sister? Or was he the man in this apartment, entertaining high-brow corporate colleagues? Was he the business magnate, or the loving, protective brother? Was he Cecilia's boss, or the man who would have fought today to ensure her safety?

He was the same Linc and yet not the same—because the Linc of six years ago had rejected her interest in him. *This* Linc had kissed her, held her and he was letting himself care about her. He *was*!

Cecilia told herself he must be all of those people, all of those things. His complexity had caught her attention from the first day they'd met, and it intrigued her more and more now as she came to know each new layer of him in a more personal way.

Cecilia made her call to the correctional centre then, and they surprised her by allowing her to speak to Stacey.

'Cecilia? What's going on? Are you okay?' Panic

rang in Stacey's tone when she came on the line. 'People don't get called to the phone here unless it's bad news, and on top of that they moved me into the strict protection section here today!'

'I'm afraid it *is* troubling news, Stacey.' Cecilia drew a breath and explained what had happened. 'I've been to the police, and obviously the staff there at the centre know about it as well now. I'm glad they've moved you. I was trying not to worry about whether harm could come to you. '

'It won't. Not in that way, now that I've been shifted. But this is still my worst nightmare.' Stacey's words were low. 'And I've brought it down not only on myself but on you. I'm so sorry, Cecilia.'

'We're going to be okay, Stacey. We can get through this together.' She had to tell her sister what she'd discovered about this man. 'There's more you need to know. Joe has warrants out in New Zealand for offences the police described as "both violent and serious", as well as for the robbery here.'

'Are you completely sure about this?' Stacey's voice shook as she asked the question.

Cecilia's heart ached for her sister so much in that moment. 'I'm quite sure.'

'He needs to be caught.' There was a pause and then Stacey spoke again. 'There are things I can tell the authorities that might help them to track him down. Cee, I know you may not believe me, but I thought he and I were going to have a life together. That sounds ludicrous now, but I thought he was someone different.'

'I understand, Stacey. Please don't give up on yourself because this has happened.'

'I won't.' Determination fuelled Stacey's words. 'If I do that, then I'll be letting him get away with how he used me.'

Cecilia was grateful to hear the words but knew her sister would need to hold on to her determination as hard as she could. 'I love you, Stacey.'

They talked for a minute or two more, until Cecilia was finally able to put the phone down.

She turned to Linc, and all the pent-up emotion surfaced. 'She's going to work with the police to try and help them catch him.'

'That's good.'

He handed her the cup of tea and settled beside her on the sofa with his coffee. His calmness helped her to centre herself again.

'She's not a criminal.' It was a relief to say it and to let it sink into her own heart. 'Stacey has a great deal of passion for life, but deep down she has a good heart.'

'Something tells me that with you to help her, she'll find her way back to the best of herself in time.'

'Thank you, Linc—for helping me with these issues.' She went on, 'Most people wouldn't even want to try to understand what it's like to have to deal with a person you care about being incarcerated, let alone today's problems.'

'I understand more than you know.' His words were low.

'What do you mean?'

How could he understand more? For a moment she wasn't sure if he would answer, but then he spoke.

'My brothers and I had a great deal of our freedom taken from us when we were growing up.' His gaze fell to his hands for a moment. 'Being stuck in an orphanage, with no option to get away until we were old enough to leave under our own steam. Scant meals, and all of them identical. I know it's not the same as your sister's situation, but it had a strong impact on each of us.'

'How did that happen to you—to them?' She knew Linc and the other two weren't blood brothers, yet their love for each other was as strong as hers for Stacey. His brothers even carried his last name now.

'Brent's father thought he was a disappointment.' Linc's words were low, edged with harshness, as though even to say it, let alone reveal that it had happened to Brent, infuriated him. 'In my case my mother had died and my father was an alcoholic. He didn't want the responsibility of raising a child so he dumped me at the orphanage.'

'Like our mother leaving Stacey and me…' There was an oddly comforting affinity in knowing that she and Linc held this common bond. 'In our case she waited until we finished school, but even that much was a strain for her—and she didn't hold back in letting us know that.'

'Regardless of their age, no person deserves to be treated that way.'

Linc said this with finality, just as his brother Alex buzzed to come up, and Linc got up and punched a code into a number pad on the wall to allow Alex access.

Minutes later Linc's youngest brother stepped into Linc's apartment, clapped his brother on the back and turned his attention to Cecilia. 'You're all right? Linc said there was a bit of a shake-up with some guy threatening you.'

'I'm fine. Thank you, Alex.'

In that moment Cecilia knew that Linc hadn't exposed any more of her story than had been necessary. She valued Linc for that but couldn't help wondering why he'd left Alex out of his explanation about the orphanage.

Cecilia forced her attention back to Linc's brother. 'It was good of you and Brent to go to my home and collect Linc's car.'

The brothers might have grown up in difficult circumstances, but it appeared to have brought out the best in all of them.

Cecilia's glance shifted to the man holding her thoughts, and her heart softened despite herself.

Linc's gaze locked with hers, and for a moment she thought she saw deep emotion churning in his eyes.

Seconds later he'd looked away, and Alex's calm words filled what Cecilia hadn't noticed yet was a silence.

'So you're okay, big brother?' The younger man glanced from one to the other of them. His gaze finally settled on Linc. 'There's nothing else I can do for you? I could ask Jayne to come over for a while to visit with Cecilia. Brent's waiting in the parking area, but I can get him up here now, too, if needed.'

'I've got it covered.' Linc's face softened. 'But thanks.'

'You'll both be safe here for as long as necessary. I know nothing will happen. It's just—' Alex headed for the door. 'Aw, well, you know... Anyway, if you need anything, you know I'll come in an instant.

As will Brent. Keep us informed of developments, please.'

Linc stopped him before he got through the door and clasped his shoulder for a long moment. 'I know, and I will. Say hi to Jayne.'

Alex's glance drifted to Cecilia for a moment and then back to his brother. 'See you later.'

The day passed. There were further conversations with the police, and then Cecilia and Linc prepared an early evening meal together. Linc proved a dab hand with pasta and confided that he'd worked for a time in a restaurant when he'd been trying to amass enough resources to get his brothers out of the orphanage and make his business empire strong enough that he could afford to support them.

He seemed sad as he spoke.

'You never mentioned how Alex ended up in the orphanage.' Cecilia carried her plate to the outdoor dining seating on Linc's balcony.

'We never knew.' Linc pushed his food around on his plate.

Cecilia tried to give her attention to the meal. The food was delicious, the wine Linc had poured to go with it beautifully refreshing. Yet she really couldn't do the food justice. Linc seemed to be struggling, too.

'Not hungry?' Linc asked of Cecilia and wished he could take the strain from her slender shoulders.

She shook her head. 'It's delicious, Linc, but I keep thinking about all that's happened today and about families and the difficulties they face. I hate thinking how hard it must have been for you and your brothers.'

'For you and your sister, too, by the sounds of it.'

He set down his fork and, by silent mutual consent, they moved back inside. This time when she settled on the sofa, he sat right beside her.

He went on. 'It sounds as though both of you needed your mother's support and missed out on it.'

'Yes.' That was certainly true. 'I ended up trying to be a mother to Stacey, and that hasn't always worked out well for our relationship with each other. You know, this has been a rough day, and I'm worried about what's ahead. I *have* to go back to work tomorrow. There's just too much to be done.'

'You would have managed on your own today if you'd had to, but I'm glad to have been able to help. And we'll see how things are going tomorrow when tomorrow arrives.'

His fingers threaded through hers. It was just that—such a simple thing—but Cecilia sighed and closed her eyes and he drew her head onto his shoulder as they sat there side by side.

She needed this comfort more than she ever would have wanted to admit. So she took it and let herself absorb the healing it brought.

That it would shift from comfort to something more than that was inevitable. Cecilia knew it, and when Linc turned his head, she met him halfway—wanting this, wanting *him*.

Outside, night was falling over the city, and there was a man on the loose somewhere who'd threatened her and who had to be caught.

But here in Linc's apartment Cecilia was safe, and she lost herself in Linc's kiss. That kiss became another. And another.

As their lips meshed, tenderness for him swept

through her and she received tenderness from him. That tenderness brought healing from the most overwhelming aspects of the day they had both shared. Fears receded to a more manageable level. Gratitude was registered and remembered, and then placed aside to allow her to focus wholly on these precious shared kisses with a man who was perhaps also becoming precious to her.

She'd asked herself where a relationship between them might go. Tonight there was desire and need and tender emotion, and she wanted all of those things with Linc. She wanted that beginning. Cecilia didn't let herself think of where such a beginning might lead.

'I have longed for this more than you can know.' Linc's words were low.

His fingers sifted through her hair, and his hand came to rest on the nape of her neck. A shiver of pleasure followed his touch.

She cupped his cheek and, when the kiss deepened, gripped his strong upper arm and allowed delight and need to blend in the giving and returning of each breathless moment. Cecilia could have continued like that forever, and yet she wanted more. So much more.

'Cecilia...'

Oh, so much was expressed in that simple speaking of her name, in a voice that had deepened and mellowed with all they had shared.

Yet there was a question there—a silent seeking of agreement.

Yes, Linc. Yes, with all that I have and all that I am. Yes.

The response was deep within her soul, surpassing any conscious thought of warning to herself that she might have formulated. She couldn't have denied that 'yes' if she'd tried.

And there were no thoughts of warning or caution or 'what ifs' or concerns. There was this and only this, and her heart was engaged.

She acknowledged that in this moment she should gently extract herself, end this here, cherish these shared kisses and seek nothing more. But Cecilia could only focus on the desire for her that glowed in the depths of Linc's eyes, on all the emotions she felt within herself, both named and unnamed, and on the soft and gentle expression on his face. On the touch of his hands that now cupped her shoulders and stroked her face.

'Take me to your room, Linc.'

Linc heard Cecilia's words, saw the need and longing reflected in her eyes, and faced a watershed moment deep within himself.

He had turned his back six years ago, for her sake, because he'd known he would never truly commit. Now Linc knew that his emotions *were* invested in Cecilia, that his feelings were real and only for her.

Linc wanted to give her those things, but would she be able to receive them and let it end there without being hurt? For that matter, could he give in that way and end it without hurt to his own emotions?

Too late, Linc. You're already there.

Deep down he knew that, and he hoped for this chance to just this once do all that he could to show her those feelings.

'I need you, Cecilia, and I need this night. But I can't… In terms of the future…' His chest hurt and he struggled to go on.

'I don't care, Linc. I need—' She broke off, and her gaze was clear and determined as it held his.

Thank you. With all my heart and soul, thank you.

Linc took Cecilia's hand and drew her from the sofa. It felt like the most natural and right thing to lead her to the door of his room.

He drew Cecilia inside with him, turned her into his arms and lowered his mouth to hers once again, knowing that now there would be more. There would be the fulfilment of all the desire that hummed in the air surrounding them, the opportunity to cherish and give and revere.

He gave himself to making it the most special experience for her that he possibly could. Valuing her with all he could invest in that valuing. Expressing without words the emotions running through the fabric of his soul.

If you don't say it, it's not real.

The childhood words were silly, because these emotions were entirely real, whether they were verbalised or not. Yet they couldn't be spoken because he couldn't look for a future.

Linc didn't ask himself in that moment just what those deep emotions meant. He wasn't sure he could afford to know. Instead, he breathed deeply and inhaled Cecilia's closeness and let it fill him.

Linc gave himself to these shared and treasured pleasures, this precious giving and receiving. He was all of himself and yet more within himself than he had ever been. That was all Linc knew—that and the deep, resonating need to demonstrate to Cecilia how much sharing this with her meant to him.

His breath caught as she melted wholly into his

embrace. His arms trembled with how deeply he valued holding her. Chest to chest, warmth shared, soft lips against caressing lips, they explored as people who knew each other but didn't really, and now they needed so much more.

Today had acted as a catalyst for him. He felt as though layers had been peeled from his soul and that he could finally acknowledge that he *did* long for Cecilia. That he did not simply *want* but *needed* to carry their closeness to this inevitable conclusion.

Linc needed this with everything within him. Just once…and only with her…

'Linc…' She whispered his name against his lips.

He swept her closer and gave all his being to the *sense* of her—the soft loveliness of her arms about his neck and the delicate arch of her spine where his hands held her. She pressed closer still. She seemed unable to be near enough.

Something inside Linc, in some place that he hadn't known before, felt *right* for the first time in his life. *This was right*—holding her, sharing these precious moments.

His chest rose and fell on a deep breath. He pushed away the thought that there could never be this again—pushed it far, far away, where it couldn't tighten its grip until he could no longer breathe, where he might not feel it even existed any more.

'Cecilia…' He murmured her name against her lips and grounded his emotions in this giving.

'Oh, Linc…'

My heart is so full of emotion for you right now.

Cecilia couldn't speak the words, but they rose in her mind as she embraced Linc and he embraced her.

Everything about these moments imbued her with thoughts and emotions so deep she couldn't fathom how she could feel so much.

Impossible to try to stop herself, to protect those emotions. So she told herself not to label them, not to give them names—because while they were nebulous and unnamed she could have this and not think about tomorrow...

Linc's hand rose to stroke her hair. 'Your hair is beautiful. It's so soft.'

He murmured the words before his lips touched hers again.

'I want this.'

Conviction echoed in her quiet words. Her hand rose to his chest, felt its strong rise and fall as he registered her words.

She went on. 'I want to share this—with you. Everything there is to share...' Everything that could be shared from her emotions to his.

He'd made no promises, had been careful that she understood there would be no tomorrow. And Cecilia did understand, and it made this easier. One chance to give and receive and close a chapter. She would feel happy because of that.

Surely she would...

His hands stroked her arms reverently, with the lightest touch against her skin, and she let go of the uneasy thought.

As clothing fell away she felt only a sense of rightness so strong and so comforting that it was infinitely beautiful finally to become one with him. Every barrier was removed and only this existed.

He held her tenderly and his gaze locked with hers.

Each touch seemed to value her deeply, each moment of delight seemed to bring them closer.

Time ceased to exist. Nothing existed but the two of them. His touch. Their shared kisses. And more…

A crescendo built—until finally she looked deep into his eyes and felt that their souls must have merged as they yielded together.

Held in his arms in the afterglow, Cecilia asked herself how she could feel as though her world had stopped still and as if Linc held the key to all that she was and would ever be. This didn't feel like 'closure' from her six-year-old feelings.

Inside her was a burgeoning emotion. It spread through her heart until she felt overtaken by it. She realised in that moment that she had fallen deeply and irrevocably in love with Linc. Rather than having closed the chapter, she had unleashed this.

The knowledge was so large, so all-encompassing, that she thought he must surely sense it. She tensed, and her breath stopped. Because he mustn't know. Not now. Not until she could come to terms with this and know how to deal with it.

She *loved* him! Loved him in a way that would dictate her wanting to be with him and be part of his life forever. No, not just part. She would want to be right there in the centre of his world, and him in hers, living out life *together*.

Linc gave a deep sigh and drew her gently closer, encouraging her to curl into his arms. He seemed close to sleep as he placed a soft kiss in her hair.

'Your hair is beautiful. It's so soft.'

The echo of his earlier words reverberated.

She thought he'd also whispered that she humbled him, that he didn't know himself right then.

She realised that Hugh was the chapter that had been closed completely. That had been a weak shadow of real emotion in the first place, and it was now so completely gone. She had wanted true love, but Hugh had not been that.

Cecilia understood this now because of the man who held her and the love she held for him.

How would she face tomorrow?

She closed her eyes and willed the thought away.

Exhaustion won out at long last.

She slept.

CHAPTER TEN

'I SHOULD BE at the nursery, making sure my staff are safe and continuing with preparations for the masked ball.'

Cecilia spoke with emphasis as she addressed her words to the small group gathered in the rooftop garden area at Linc's family's warehouse building the next morning.

'How can I hide myself away and leave them vulnerable?'

It was still early. Linc had called this family meeting to put the situation to his brothers and sisters-in-law and seek their collective input.

Cecilia had agreed to the meeting. In truth, it had seemed easier than trying to deal with her new-found emotions alone with Linc at his city apartment. But those emotions were still there, and so were the demands of the rest of her life.

It was clear Linc wanted to gain his family's support in convincing her to stay out of the limelight. Linc had said as much when he'd woken that morning and joined her in his kitchen, where she'd been already showered, dressed and waiting to tell him she *had* to go to work.

All the shock and uncertainty she had been too exhausted to process late last night, in those incredulous moments when she had realised she'd fallen in love with Linc, had awoken her before dawn, determined to make themselves well and truly known again and demand that she work out what to do about them.

As she'd showered and dressed, a need to be by herself and process this new knowledge had overwhelmed her to such a degree that she hadn't known how she could even face Linc.

She loved him.

There could be no future for them.

Her heart was breaking.

All her heart and emotions, everything she had inside her, had fallen in love with one amazing man. That was the beautiful part…the wonderful, incredible part.

But Linc hadn't expressed those emotions—had not at any point in time led her to believe that he had fallen for her. On the contrary, he had tried not to yield to the deepening attraction and interest between them, and last night he had warned her…

She had to acknowledge that if they'd not been through such an emotionally charged day yesterday, in all likelihood he would have continued to avoid taking things further between them.

And his succumbing to temptation did not mean that his emotions had changed whatsoever. That part shattered her heart all over again.

Cecilia caught his gaze. Oh, it was so hard now to look into the grey eyes that had looked into hers in the very moments before she'd realised she loved him!

The only thing Cecilia could think of to do was

hiding herself in her work and finding distance from him so she could shore up her defences.

'Linc, you said yourself that you've assigned a security team to the nursery, so there shouldn't be any problems with me going back to work today.'

You have to let me go. I can't be in your company—especially not just the two of us, shut away from the world. Not yet. Not now. Not ever. And I can't think of that right now, either!

She needed to gather her strength and figure out how to go forward from here.

'I should be safe enough at the nursery with a security detail in place. And if I'm not, then my staff aren't, either!'

This was a genuine concern, and it made complete sense to her.

Until Jayne spoke.

'I have to agree with Linc.' Concern for Cecilia shone in Jayne's eyes. 'At least for today allow the security team at the nursery to monitor things and give some feedback as to whether anything odd or unusual occurs. It would be better if you didn't go back to your workplace, Cecilia. You'd be distracting them from being able to watch the others as well as they would without you there.'

Cecilia's hopes fell. 'I hadn't considered that...'

She *should* have considered that. It should have been completely obvious to her.

Linc heard Cecilia respond to Jayne's comment and silently thanked his sister-in-law for voicing the concerns that he shared. But Cecilia looked so crestfallen as she acknowledged Jayne's point, and—as they had done since he'd first woken that morning—

Linc's emotions churned. He'd thought that he could give himself last night. That if he made sure Cecilia understood there would be no tomorrow it would be okay. He'd convinced himself he could do it without causing hurt, provided he was honest about it at the start.

If all that was true, then why did he feel so empty inside right now? Why did he feel that he'd lost something wonderful? And Cecilia... She didn't look happy and fulfilled—as though she'd been able to answer a question that had been in her mind and now could happily move on. She looked as though she wanted to run as far and as fast as she could.

What if she did? What if she took up the offer from the Silver Bells committee and left him?

You mean if she left working for you.

Either would have the same result. She would disappear out of his life, and he wouldn't see her any more.

Panic tightened Linc's chest. He couldn't let that happen!

So help her sort out these issues and, the first chance you get, talk to her about last night. Tell her how it made you feel. Tell her you want more.

But Linc couldn't *have* more. He glanced across the room at his brothers. He could *not* have more.

'It's still early.' Linc offered the words quietly.

There was still the situation of a dangerous man who had threatened harm to Cecilia, and that situation had to be managed, whether Linc had other things preying on his mind or not.

So he waited until Cecilia finally raised her gaze to his, and then he said, 'We have time to contact Jemmie, to let her know the basics of the situation and ask her if she'll be comfortable taking charge for today while the security team do their thing. I am confident she and the others will be protected if anything does transpire.'

'I have to work.' Cecilia's words held an agitated edge. 'It's not that I believe the nursery can't get along without me—certainly for one day, anyway— although the timing isn't great. I just can't spend the day in idleness with nothing to do but think.'

The others would believe she wanted to avoid thinking about the man on the loose, her sister's plight and of course those things *would* be causing her worry and stress. And she *would* think about them if left to her own devices.

Somehow Linc had lost sight of that for a bit— had failed to remember all the pressure that would be weighing on Cecilia's shoulders today.

He felt selfish in that moment, to have believed all her thoughts would be of what they had shared. Last night he could have controlled that situation—not allowed it to reach the conclusion it had.

Yet even as he thought this, Linc knew it wasn't true. For the first time in his life he had *not* been able to fight his way out of core emotions that had been so strong.

Cecilia sought his gaze and held it. 'You know I need to be at work. I can't possibly— I need—'

'Whatever you need, you will have. I will make this work for you, Cecilia.'

He simply made that commitment to her. Linc was a man who'd struggled, triumphed, lost, loved, given and been blessed beyond anything he'd imagined his life could be. The family he, Alex and Brent had built out of the ashes of abandonment had saved Linc.

If Cecilia needed space, he could give her that and still keep her secure. He could help her, even while he tried to sort out his own emotions.

Linc felt a degree of calmness return as he realised he could do this.

Cecilia heard Linc's words and felt the kindness and care in them. Oh, she wanted so much to believe that those words came out of a deeply held love for her, but she knew Linc would do this even if they had never shared so much as a kiss.

Don't think about it. Not yet.

She glanced about at the gathered group. 'I'm grateful to all of you. None of you needed to weigh in on this but you did so without hesitating, and that means the world to me. I just—' For one panicky moment she thought she might choke into tears in front of them all. 'I need—'

'Not to have everything taken away at once?' Brent broke in.

'Not to feel overwhelmed with pressure?' Fiona added. She turned her gaze towards Linc. 'You're quite certain everyone at the nursery will be safe?'

'I don't believe anyone could get past the teams that are in place.' Linc's words were resolute. 'But I still have to take every precaution, and because the guy threatened Cecilia directly, made it clear his grudge is towards her specifically, I can't make that same guarantee for her.'

When he went on, it was as though he had focused inwardly.

'I've made the mistake in the past of letting a bully

harm someone—' He broke off and his gaze rested on Alex. 'That was unforgivable, and I will not ever allow it to happen again.'

'That was a long time ago, and it wasn't even your—' Alex got halfway to his feet.

'Worry about it later, Alex.' Brent cut him off almost sharply. 'We need to focus on the current issue.'

What had Linc meant? And why had his words caused Alex to respond in that way, and Brent to cut the conversation off completely?

Brent spoke again before Cecilia could think any further. 'We've established that the security team should be able to cope and that they'll need at least today to observe without the bulk of their attention being on keeping Cecilia safe.'

'Yeah. We have.' Linc turned his gaze to Cecilia. 'I'm sorry, but that's where I stand on it. I'd shut the place down rather than have you there today.'

She knew that he would, and she paused to consider and then reject that option. 'I'd rather avoid that, if possible. It would only draw more attention to the fact that there's a problem.'

'I have what I hope will be a tolerable second option for you.'

As Linc spoke the words he could only be grateful for his family and for the support they'd given by rallying around this morning. Last night had thrown him so far off balance he'd been concerned that he might miss something or make a poor decision.

Linc didn't feel worried about that any more, but he was still thankful.

'I'll bring some of your repurposing items here. You can work on them today and stay for as long as is needed. You'll have access to the phone and internet, so you'll be able to give support to Jemmie remotely, as well.'

This apartment was large. They could work all day and barely see each other if they chose.

'Great idea.' Brent nodded his approval.

'We can take turns coming here if you need to go away anywhere, Linc.' Alex added his thoughts.

'I'll agree to that plan—for today at least.' Cecilia didn't love it, but if she could busy herself that would help. She caught each person's gaze in turn. 'Thank you all for—for caring.'

At least by accepting this today, she would ensure that Linc's relatives didn't do dangerous things such as turning up at the plant nursery, where protection would be more difficult, wanting to express their support for her. Given their care and concern this morning, she wouldn't put it past them!

'Being able to do my repurposing here would be ideal—just while we're waiting to see how the security team are feeling about things.' She filled her tone with determination.

'Thanks, everyone. Why don't we make a start on breakfast?' It was Linc who made the suggestion. 'I'll head to the nursery to collect some of Cecilia's items. I've got the truck downstairs. I haven't had it out for a while. It will be a good chance to give it a run and for me to check in with the security team at the same time.'

'You'll keep safe?'

Cecilia wanted to go with him but knew that he wasn't inviting her and that he wouldn't do so. She had to stay out of the limelight, whether she wanted to or not.

'I'll phone Jemmie and bring her up to speed.'

'Remember that you don't have to tell her about anything more than the threat itself if you don't want to.' Linc turned the grey-eyed gaze on her that was now so familiar and dear. His words were protective, but perhaps only she could hear that? Or was she making it up because she wanted to believe it?

A moment later Linc had gone, and Cecilia was left with his loving, amazing family, all examining her with interested gazes.

'Will you excuse me if I step away to make the call to my assistant manager?' She grasped at this plan a little desperately and hoped her emotions—the ones that related to Linc, at least—weren't all over her face.

Hopefully, Linc wouldn't be gone too long.

Hopefully, Cecilia would soon get control over these new feelings for Linc that had thrown her so profoundly off balance. Maybe she only *thought* she felt this way due to the stress of the current circumstances?

Dream on, Cecilia.

Fine—then she would focus on what had to be done today, one step and one moment at a time, until sooner or later she would get some time to herself and figure out how to deal with these feelings, protecting herself from heartbreak in the process. There had to be a way.

Cecilia stepped away and phoned Jemmie.

CHAPTER ELEVEN

'THEY NEED TO catch this guy.'

Cecilia spoke the words after jumping when the fridge in Linc's kitchen gave a shuddering sound at the end of its auto-defrost cycle.

She went on. 'Either that or I'm going to turn into a complete, neurotic mess.'

It was the following evening. They'd agreed that they would go in to the plant nursery for the day that morning.

Doing so hadn't been as easy as Cecilia had thought it would be. She'd spent all day looking over her shoulder and worrying. Was everyone safe? Could the security team really cope, no matter what happened? Was Stacey truly safe in the correctional facility? What if Linc was holding off talking about the night they'd shared because he didn't want to let her down when she was relying on staying at his home until she could be safe elsewhere?

And so it had gone—all of yesterday and even more today—until finally they'd returned to his apartment to a dinner prepared and left for them by Linc's housekeeper, Rosa.

Cecilia was once again only picking at her food.

There seemed to be a permanent lump lodged in her throat.

Linc watched Cecilia push food around her plate and couldn't deny the relief of having her back here, where it was a whole lot easier to keep an eye on her. All except for the fact that they were now alone, and he'd had all day today and all of yesterday to think about what they'd shared, and all he'd been able to think was what if he'd made such a mess of things that he couldn't turn that around?

'You've got every right to be jumpy.' He stood, cleared their plates and they made their way to the living room.

'I had a call from Stacey today.' She settled into an armchair as he took his place on the sofa. 'It came through while you were doing a check with the security team.'

'How was she?'

'She's okay. She's had several conversations with the police.' Cecilia paused and worried at her lip with her teeth. 'It's been done discreetly, and she's really hoping what she's told them will help them catch the guy.'

'You never stop thinking about her, do you?' It was an observation as well as a question.

'Only when—' Cecilia stopped and shook her head. 'Stacey's very important to me,' she said instead. 'That will never change. I know it's the same for you with Brent and Alex. You love them deeply.'

Her voice held a hint of wistful longing, but all Linc heard was praise for his caring nature. He didn't want to tell her the truth, and yet he couldn't withhold it.

You'll lose her. She won't want you if you tell her what happened. It will be one more rejection in your life, and this time you'll deserve it.

'I *do* love Brent and Alex.' At least he could say that much with absolute assurance. He forced himself to go on. 'But there was a time when I abandoned Alex. He suffered because of my self-interest—because I put what I wanted before making sure he was okay.'

'I can't imagine that, Linc.' Surprise tinged her words.

Linc felt ill. He'd been asking himself how he could hold on to Cecilia, but he knew he didn't have the right to that kind of wonderful relationship. He shouldn't have allowed himself to ignore that fact. Not for a moment.

'I ignored him for weeks on end when he was at his most vulnerable and needed me to be there for him.'

'What—what happened?' Concern filled her expression.

'I was the oldest, and as a result the first to leave the orphanage—though I was able to get Brent out soon after. I got Brent a job. Alex, because he was younger...'

'He had to wait before he could join you?' Her expression showed empathy. 'It must have been tough, having to leave him there?'

'It wasn't as tough for me as it should have been.'

Linc had never discussed this. Not even with Brent, back when it had all unfolded. Not his emotions about it. He hadn't needed to say anything. He'd done something profoundly selfish and wrong, and he'd shoved that acknowledgment deep down inside himself where it would never leave him. Where it belonged.

'I was so focused on making money as fast as I could. Instead of paying attention to what was happening to Alex, I let weeks go by without checking on him.'

He'd allowed the old adage of 'out of sight, out of mind' to take hold in him.

Cecilia's expression sobered. 'Go on.'

'Brent had been keeping closer contact with Alex, but he got some work that took him away for a month.' Here Linc's eyes clouded over, as though in remembered pain. 'He came and saw me one night and asked me to make sure I visited Alex often. Brent was worried about a new employee the orphanage had taken on. He thought the man could be violent. With him going away, he knew he couldn't keep an eye on him.'

'Oh, Linc...' Cecilia wasn't sure that she *did* want to know the rest.

'I checked on Alex just once—asked if he was doing okay.' Linc shook his head. 'I asked him if he'd mind if I didn't come in much because I was so busy. He didn't want me to worry or feel I had to leave my work because of him, so he told me everything was fine.'

'But it wasn't?' Cecilia almost whispered the words.

Linc forced the rest out. 'When I finally visited Alex again, he was trying to hide that his ribs were bruised.' Linc closed his eyes for a moment. 'That man had beaten Alex where he knew no person would be able to see it. He'd done it because he was mean and because he could—and I'd allowed it to happen.

I didn't listen when Brent expressed his concerns, and I put it on Alex to tell me whether something was wrong or not. And he didn't want to stop me being able to work.'

The self-condemnation and the agony of what had occurred while Linc should have been on watch were rife in his tone as well as in his words.

'Oh, Linc. You must have been devastated.' She offered the words carefully, and she had to add, 'But surely you know that might have happened even if you *were* visiting? Unfortunately, there are people in this world who do such things any chance they get.'

'I took Alex straight out of there, of course.' Linc said it as though there couldn't possibly have been any other option. 'I walked him out on the spot and consequences be damned. Brent and I kept him hidden until he was old enough that the authorities couldn't take him from us. It was only a few months. Why didn't I do that in the first place?'

'Because you didn't know.'

Cecilia could only imagine how he must have felt—how hard it must have been for Linc to face Brent as well, knowing that he'd failed to give the situation the attention he should have at the time.

'You removed Alex from the threat as soon as you could. That was a *good* thing.'

'Yeah, but way too late.' Linc shook his head, as though that just hadn't been enough. 'He'd been beaten for trying to protect one of the smaller kids.'

'You know, none of us are infallible—'

'Not like this.' His tone was harsh and filled with self-directed censure. 'I left my brother there to be harmed—and I did it even though Brent had brought his concerns to my attention. Thanks to me, Alex ended up being preyed on by that guy. And it wasn't just about the physical beating. There are emotional scars from things like that, which last much longer.'

Had Linc and Alex talked about this? Did Alex blame Linc? Cecilia couldn't imagine that. In fact, she was convinced that Alex not only would have forgiven him long ago, but that he would never have blamed Linc in the first place.

'It sounds to me as though Alex had the bravery to step in where a lot of other young boys wouldn't have to protect the other children.'

'I guess that's the irony.' Linc glanced at his hands before his gaze met hers again. 'Brent and me, we raised him well in there. His ethics were rock solid.'

Yet Linc couldn't let himself experience anything that resembled forgiveness for his own actions. Cecilia could see that very clearly now.

His words as he went on confirmed it. 'It was way too easy for me to forget about him. I've had to conclude it's a character flaw in myself.' He drew a breath. 'There's something wrong—wrong in me—to make me able to do that. They chose to become my brothers, and I let them down. I don't deserve the kind of happiness they've found.'

Cecilia realised in that moment that this was Linc's morning-after talk. He'd gone away and thought about what they'd shared, and he'd ruled out the possibility of any kind of a future for them because this part of his history was insurmountable for him. He couldn't forgive himself. He believed there was a flaw in his make-up that made him unworthy.

Oh, Linc. How could you believe that about your-self when you're such a good person?

Yes, he'd made a mistake—but people did that. He'd been young! He'd also been breaking himself, trying to secure things so they could all be safe, so he could make a life for all of them outside of their horrid upbringing.

Had Linc thought about and longed for a future with Cecilia as she had with him? Was that why he was saying all this now?

Cecilia couldn't let herself think that he was saying it because he'd realised how she felt about him.

As she hesitated, trying to formulate words, trying to know what to say, to understand where she stood and try to figure out what to do, Linc got to his feet.

'I had to tell you.' He seemed to be experiencing a deep pain but also to be resolute. He drew a breath. 'The time we shared together was the most precious I've experienced in my life, but I shouldn't have allowed it to happen and…and I can't let it happen again. You understand why now. You deserve more. I hope you'll forgive me.'

Linc left the room.

'We may still have no news on our wanted man, but I *can* give you some good news about the nursery.' Linc spoke the words the following day as he sat back from his computer.

They were in Cecilia's small office at the plant nursery. Cecilia wasn't as jumpy as she'd been the day before. Maybe she should have been, but she'd had very little sleep…and her heart hurt. She suspected that if she let herself feel everything to the depths that she could at the moment, she might break down.

She'd made her decision. There was no other choice that she could see. Her love for Linc would never be returned. She was trying to accept it, to be grateful that he didn't know how she felt. But mostly she was just trying to hold a great wall of pain at bay.

What news could Linc have? They were going ahead with the masked ball. They hadn't told anyone other than their staff about the issues going on. If need be, they would bring in the biggest contingent of undercover security any place had ever seen, but they *would* go ahead.

Cecilia couldn't actually think of any other good news to do with the nursery. She had news for Linc that would affect the nursery, but she doubted he would want to hear that. Then again, maybe it would be an answer to his prayers.

She forced her gaze up and away from her inspection of the catering lists spread across the desk in front of her. It wasn't easy to look at Linc, but she did it.

'What is it?'

'I've finished the review, and it should be no surprise to you that everything's fine.' He drew a breath. 'I'm more than happy to agree to the percentage share in the nursery that you proposed when you initially approached me about doing this review.'

For a moment she simply didn't comprehend his words—and then they sank in.

'I'm grateful for that, Linc, truly I am...'

She fought to say the rest of the words that needed to be said and to keep her chin up while she did it. Now was the perfect time. So she went on.

'But I won't be taking the offer up after all.'

She couldn't stay here—be here while Linc reverted to stopping in periodically, expecting her update calls as he'd done before this review had started. It wouldn't matter whether those visits took place weekly or were months apart. Or that those phone calls would be all about business. She would hurt a little more each time she saw him. Because loving someone who didn't share those feelings would do that to her.

Cecilia understood his self-blame over his brother, his belief that he wasn't deserving of love. But she *did* love him. And it hurt her every single moment to know that in the end he simply didn't share those feelings.

If he did, he would fight for her, whether he regretted his past or not.

'I thought you were just keeping a presence here today because of the safety issues—though I am pleased about the review results.' She met his gaze. 'It's just that I've decided to take up the offer from the Silver Bells flower show committee. I'm going to work for them. Actually, I'm planning to leave here as soon as the masked ball is over. In the end…it's best. I'm— It's an exciting new opportunity for me, really.'

She felt like two people. The one sitting there, saying those words and trying to appear calm, as though this was what she wanted to do, and the one who loved Linc and was being torn apart by that love.

'If this is because—' Linc's words were strained.

'I've just realised I'm ready for a change.' She pushed the lie past her teeth. This was harder than she had thought it would be, and she prayed that she wouldn't break down.

Linc got to his feet. 'I—I wish you well. Would you excuse me, Cecilia? I need—'

He didn't say what it was that he needed. Linc simply left the room.

CHAPTER TWELVE

'IT LOOKS GOOD, LINC.'

Alex made the comment as he and Linc stood back from the area in the centre of Fleurmazing's signature maze, which now held a fully constructed and functional raised and canopied dais, in readiness for the masked ball that would commence three hours from now.

'People are going to love it. And you can relax now, knowing that guy has been caught.'

When Alex had learned that Linc was planning to assist with the construction of the dais, he'd put his hand up to come along and help. Linc hadn't really wanted the company, yet Alex's presence had done him good.

Now the construction was finished, and it was just the two of them admiring the result of their handiwork.

Linc glanced at Alex. 'He was picked up in New Zealand. He'll face charges and do jail time over there. It's looking like at least a decade of accumulated charges.'

'He won't be allowed back into Australia after that.' Alex said it with certainty. 'How's Cecilia taking all of this?' His gaze focused on the maze beyond the dais as he went on. 'She must feel as though she's been put through a wringer, one way and another.'

'What do you mean by that?' Linc asked the question too quickly before he realised Alex probably meant nothing at all beyond the comment itself. 'Sorry. It's been a tense time. Cecilia is visiting her sister this afternoon at the correctional centre. I'm sure she's relieved the guy's been caught.'

'You don't sound real convinced about her state of happiness, brother.'

Those words drew Linc's gaze to Alex, and he saw his younger brother was looking right at him now.

Alex searched his face. 'Yet seeing the two of you together just days ago, I would have thought maybe both of you were on the brink of something special.'

Linc didn't even ask himself how Alex had discerned that. 'I'm not enough for her. She's better off without me.'

'That's the most foolish rubbish I've heard in all the time I've known you.' Alex's words were sharp. 'Give me one good reason for that belief.'

'When the chips are down, I just think about myself.' Linc fired the volley straight back.

He wanted to tell Alex to keep out of this and mind his own business. His heart hurt, and Alex prodding around in his emotions wasn't helping. Instead, he flayed himself with their shared past.

'You of all people ought to know that—considering you were the one who suffered thanks to my self-interest.'

Instead of backing off, Alex took a step closer to Linc to emphasise his response. 'It wasn't until recently that I even realised you blamed yourself for what happened way back when I was still in the orphanage. Brent and I always believed you were so locked down about it at the time because you were rightly angry—infuriated that such a piece of scum existed and had got into that place to smack around little kids. Just as we were.'

'He preyed on you because I failed to keep watch. I failed to protect you—'

'You're not to blame. *You* weren't the person who bullied me, who had been bullying other kids, as well.'

'I should have made time to visit you. You and Brent let me into your lives.' Linc said it with all the pain he'd carried for so long. 'You chose to accept me as a brother. I was the oldest. I had a responsibility to look after both of you, and in your case I failed.'

'You mean while you were working yourself into the ground so you'd be able to provide for me once I was old enough to leave?'

Ah, don't make me out to be a hero, Alex.

'I don't think you and Brent realise,' Linc said slowly. 'You saved me. I don't believe I could have handled that place without you both.'

He'd have died from lack of love without them. Maybe not immediately, maybe not for all his lifetime, but inside he'd have died.

Alex's gaze held his as he responded, 'We all saved each other. Do you think I shouldn't have married Jayne because I wasn't good enough for my parents to want to keep me? Or that Brent shouldn't have found happiness with Fiona because his father shoved him into that place just as yours did you? Do you think we're not good enough? Because it seems if you think that way about yourself, that's how you think about us.'

'It's not like that. You're twisting the situation.'

And yet...

'This can't just be about me punishing myself.' Linc said it slowly. 'If it is, then I've been using it as an excuse—'

To avoid something?

To avoid letting himself love in case he wasn't loved in return?

'I love her.' He uttered it with complete knowledge. 'I love Cecilia.'

And he'd pushed her away. Shoved her away hard in case—God forbid—she might love him in return. She'd handed in her resignation. After tonight she would be cut off from him.

Alex gripped his arm for a moment, and then let go. 'Brent and I both love you, Linc. We want you to be happy. Neither of us blame you for the past. You held the three of us together and you should be damn proud of that fact. Just know that the past is the past. If we can both let go of it, so should you.'

As Alex started to leave the area, he turned and a satisfied smile came over his face. 'Remember how we all went back to the orphanage the night after you got me out? It was probably wrong of us, but we were going to dish out a bit of justice of our own to that guy?'

'Yeah.' Linc remembered. 'The police were there. One of the little kids you'd protected had sneaked into the office and made the call before we could— had told them the guy was there, beating everyone.'

'The orphanage was shut down and the kids got

shifted into better situations. Most of them got placed into loving families.' Alex raised his brows. 'Do you think that would have happened if I hadn't been beaten that one time? For me, personally, I reckon that was worth it.'

Alex left then.

Linc felt humbled. And he had to ask himself: *had* he been hiding behind the guilt from his past in order to refuse to let himself look ahead and hope for the future? Had he been afraid to love because he hadn't been loved by his father?

If that was the case, had he left it too late to do something about it? Had he lost Cecilia forever?

Because in his heart of hearts he knew that he loved Cecilia with everything in him. That the idea of a life without her in it filled him with pain. That he wanted happiness with her if he could find it, and if she would be willing to take him on and try.

The masked ball was hours away.

Linc needed a plan.

He strode from the nursery.

CHAPTER THIRTEEN

'THANKS, JEMMIE, for all your help.'

Cecilia couldn't believe the evening of the masked ball was here at last. But everything was in place. Jemmie had stayed after hours to give Cecilia time to go home and change in readiness for the ball itself, but now Cecilia was back, the guests would arrive within the hour and Cecilia's heart was so torn she didn't know where to start.

Jemmie said her goodbyes and left the office. At the entrance of the nursery, members of the Silver Bells flower show committee had started to gather. They would greet the guests and send them into the maze to begin what Cecilia hoped would prove to be a magical adventure for each of them.

All Cecilia had to do was get through this night, hold it together and then...

Leave.

Make a complete new start somewhere she'd have some hope of forgetting Linc.

The pressure for tonight to be perfect was even greater because she knew she would be leaving. She wanted to give Linc this one last thing and do it really well. Not that he would see it. With the way things had gone, there was no way he would be here.

But he would hear about tonight and know she'd done a good job.

With a sigh, Cecilia stepped out into the courtyard area, locked the office door after her and made her way into the maze. It was time to go to where the dais had been raised, to check everything one last time and then, as the guests finally began to arrive, to smile and make sure each of them had a night to remember.

Cecilia lifted the delicate mask she held in one hand and placed it over her face.

Maybe it would hide her heartache.

Linc shifted from foot to foot where he stood at the edge of the dais area. He straightened his bow tie and hoped he would be able to carry this off when Cecilia arrived. It was difficult not to feel foolish wearing a mask that the woman in the shop had said made him look like—what was it?—*some swashbuckling hero*?

He just wanted to see Cecilia and to let her know that he loved her. He hoped with all his heart that she might be able to return those feelings, that he hadn't messed things up so badly he couldn't come back from it. But this night meant a lot to Cecilia, so he wanted to be sure that he looked the part.

Linc had told Cecilia about Alex. The guilt Linc had felt had been very real, but Alex had shown Linc that he'd been holding on to that past experience and blaming himself for being human. That he needed to let go of it and reach out for his own happiness. That he had to trust that he could be loved and accepted— just as Brent and Alex loved and accepted him and were themselves loved and accepted.

Behind Linc the string quartet finished tuning up

and began to play a soft, haunting melody. He had asked them to come earlier, to be ready to start playing and keep playing once Cecilia arrived.

Rosa had given him a crash course in waltzing. She'd patted his face and hadn't asked why. She was the closest thing to a mother that Linc could remember.

The rows upon rows of lights in the canopied cover above the dais came on, lending a soft glow to the fading twilight.

In that moment Cecilia stepped out of the maze and he saw her—and, oh, she looked so beautiful. A shimmering deep gold gown made her seem as one with her surroundings. Gold sandals covered her feet, and her hair was piled high on her head. Her mask of gold and blue highlighted her beautiful eyes.

She also looked fragile, as though the weight of this world sat on her shoulders.

Could she love him?

Linc's chest expanded with all the love he felt for her.

She spotted him standing there and, for just a moment, her step faltered and surprise made her eyes round.

Linc stepped down from the dais and quickly walked to greet her.

Don't leave. Don't walk away before I've had a chance to tell you—

'Cecilia. You look beautiful.'

She did. He wanted to see her in all her stages of beauty, all throughout their lives.

Her gaze searched his face. 'Thank you. I didn't think you'd be here.'

Along with the strain, did her gaze show pleasure that he was there? Or did Linc just long to see that?

'I had to come.'

As he looked at her, he knew he wanted—no, he *needed* to wake up beside her every day, forever. He needed that as much as breathing. And he hoped with all his might that she would give him that chance.

'Will you dance with me, Cecilia? Now? Before the guests start arriving?'

He held out his hand.

The string ensemble began the strains of a waltz.

Cecilia searched his face. He thought she would say no, but after a long moment she silently put her hand in his.

Linc released the breath he'd been holding and led her onto the dais. He drew Cecilia into his arms, and they circled the floor together. His arms had hurt from the lack of holding her, and now there was this symmetry, this beauty of touch and music and movement. She matched his steps perfectly, and it was effortless and so right.

He looked down into her upturned face, into the dark blue pools of her eyes, and knew that he could trust his heart in her care just as much as he wanted to care for her heart forever.

Cecilia gazed into Linc's eyes as they moved around the dance floor. She heard the quartet playing, but she saw nothing but Linc, felt nothing but the touch of his hand holding hers, his other hand against her back.

The scent of flowers kissed by the cooling night air surrounded them. Everything was perfect. She wanted to cry and never stop crying, and still she hadn't been able to deny herself this.

Oh, she had not expected to be held in Linc's arms, to be whisked about the dais as though she and no one else meant the world to him.

Please don't break my heart all over again, Linc. I don't know why you're doing this.

Why had Linc come here, asked her for this dance? She wanted to hope—and that was the most dangerous and heartbreaking thing she could do!

She'd prepared herself to leave him, to try and mend her heart away from him and, when this dance was over, that was still exactly what she had to do.

Eventually, the dance came to an end. Linc led her off the floor. 'Will you walk with me in the maze for a minute? I need to talk to you.'

'All—all right.' His serious tone made her heart thump.

'This is where I found you that first day of the review.' Linc spoke the words quietly.

She looked around her and realised they were in front of the statue of the sun goddess. Her favourite part of the maze. All of a sudden the affinity she felt with this place, with the work she'd put in, her vision and seeing her dreams come true here all welled up, and that sorrow added itself to the sorrow of unrequited love.

She started to speak before she could stop herself. 'I'll miss—'

'You remind me of her tonight.'

He spoke at the same time, and his gaze briefly rested on the statue before it returned to Cecilia.

'It's not just the colour of your dress.' He seemed

to search for words to express his thoughts. 'It's how you are inside yourself. You spread light. You warm people.'

The words weren't flattery. They were far deeper than that.

She searched his gaze. 'That's a lovely thing for you to say.'

Linc had his chance now, and he didn't want to blow it. He pulled the mask from his face and gently removed hers, dropping them both at the foot of the statue. There were some things that just couldn't be said with barriers in place.

'We've known each other for a long time...'

He started there, because that had been the start of their journey.

'Back then, when we first met...' She'd shown an interest in him and he'd rebuffed her. 'I was convinced I didn't deserve love and a happy-ever-after. I didn't know it at the time, but I was using it as an excuse.'

Linc paused for a moment. He took her hand in his and cherished the connection, the simple sense of rightness the touch gave him.

'I've realised that I *wanted* to blame myself.'

Her fingers tightened on his for an instant, and she frowned. 'Why?'

'Because it let me hold back from people other than my brothers.' He'd been afraid of being hurt. The big, strong millionaire Linc MacKay hadn't known how to protect his emotions, so he'd used that as an excuse to hold them at bay from the world. 'I didn't want to risk being given up on again, as my father gave up on me.'

'How others behave towards us can have a pro-found impact.' Cecilia's words were open and honest, and she knew she had to go on. 'Our mother telling us repeatedly that we were a burden on her not only harmed Stacey and helped her along the path of self-destruction that led her to where she is today, it also harmed me.'

It had. More than Cecilia had ever wanted to admit.

'I had very little faith that a loving relationship could be built and could last. When I tried to form one with…with Hugh, and he disappeared out of my life the moment things got challenging, it not only damaged my faith in others but my belief in myself that I was worth sticking around for.'

'And I added to that—both six years ago and recently.'

Linc's words were low, filled with remorse. Yet as he spoke, his expression became determined and his grip on her hands firmed.

'I'm in love with you, Cecilia. I'm worried sick that I've left it too late to tell you, but I love you with all my heart and I want us to be together.'

Cecilia stared at Linc mutely. All her breath seemed to have escaped from her lungs. She dragged in air. 'Wh-what did you say?'

'I love you.' The truth of it shone from his eyes. 'I'm *in love* with you. Is there any chance, Cecilia? Any chance at all that you might come to return those feelings? I want to spend the rest of my life with you. When you said you were leaving, I felt as though my world was ending.'

'Six years ago I was attracted to you…' Cecilia said it slowly, remembering that time, the immaturity of her emotions. 'But it took coming to know you closely for me to…to totally fall in love with you.'

Linc's gaze searched her face. 'I want to marry you—have children, God willing—and grow old together. I want to love you for the rest of our lives. Please tell me there's hope for that.'

Cecilia might have hesitated on the brink of Linc's proposal but, oh, she wouldn't. She simply would not—because this was worth the risk. This was worth reaching out for.

Linc was worth it.

'Yes.' She broke into a smile that was full of love and relief and happiness. 'Oh, yes, Linc. That is what I'm saying. I want all of those things, too. With *you*. It's what I want more than anything.'

'You've made me the happiest man in the world.'

The relief and acceptance in his voice showed his belief in those words. And the kiss they shared was filled with all the hope and relief and joy they both felt. Cecilia finally believed then—and, oh, it felt good to do so!

As they finally drew apart, Linc asked her, 'Will you still go to work for the Silver Bells committee?'

She searched his gaze and thought for a moment. 'Do you know, I think I will? But if you don't mind too much, I might like to take that on part-time and work on my refurbishment projects the rest of the time.'

'From our home?'

As she nodded, a smile spread over his face.

'I already do a lot of my work from home.' He looked a little sheepish. 'I'm not all that keen on the idea of working out of an office full of staff. We could work from home together…take coffee breaks and do what we liked. The warehouse—'

'Would make a perfect home for us.'

Happiness welled up inside Cecilia, and she couldn't contain it. She reached out for him, and they hugged each other for long moments before they once more drew apart.

Linc reached into his pocket and brought out a small velvet box. He dropped to one knee. His fingers shook as he opened the box and held it out to her.

'Will you marry me and accept this ring as a token of my love for you?'

Cecilia understood his vulnerability then. Knew that they could walk through life together and strengthen each other, that they truly could be stronger and greater together than either of them could ever have been on their own. Her heart opened up to all they could have and be, and she gently received the box from him.

Inside nestled a solitaire engagement ring. The band was white gold, its design cut low, to give all the attention to the glittering jewel it held.

'Oh, Linc, it's lovely.'

His quiet exhalation held both satisfaction and a hint of relief.

He got to his feet and clasped her left hand in his own. 'I'm glad you like it. I bought it today. When I saw it, I thought it was the right one for you. I had to plan, to hope you'd say yes, that it wasn't all too late. I had to put my faith on the line.'

She closed her eyes. 'Oh, Linc. I love you so. I thought I would never have the chance to tell you, let alone to think about a future together.'

'And I thought I'd lost any chance with you by being buried in fears from the past.' He blew out a breath that seemed to let the last of his tension go.

And then he slipped the ring from the box and onto her finger, and she realised it was possible that she could adore him even more.

'It fits perfectly, Linc. Like it was meant to be there. I will be proud to wear this, and every time I look at it I will remember this night and this moment.'

'The start of our future together.' Linc liked the thought a great deal.

Beyond them, they heard the murmur of the first guests entering into the beginning of the maze and knew that the masked ball was truly about to begin.

'Shall we give everyone—and ourselves—a night to remember?'

Linc retrieved their masks from where they rested at the foot of the statue.

Cecilia donned her mask and smiled a little to herself as Linc donned his and immediately took on the persona of a man of mystery.

He was *her* man now, not at all a mystery to her any more, and she liked that fact just fine.

'Yes, Linc. Let's make this a night to remember.'

They made their way back to the dance floor and, as other people arrived, one after another, the first thing they saw was a couple obviously deeply in love with each other, circling the floor in each other's arms to the strains of a beautiful waltz.

It was indeed a night to remember.

EPILOGUE

'Do you, Linc MacKay, take this woman, Cecilia Anna Tomson, to be your lawfully wedded wife?'

The celebrant's words rang out in the beautiful country chapel. She went on, adding words of love and fidelity, commitment and forever.

Cecilia stood before Linc in her wedding gown and knew that her love for him was written all over her, and she didn't care one bit that it was!

Linc's words were low and heartfelt as he responded, 'I do.'

It was Cecilia's turn then, and she saw her sister's hands shake where she stood to her left, holding Cecilia's bouquet of perfect creamy roses and baby's breath along with her own bouquet of deep red blooms. To have Stacey here, so happy herself, added to Cecilia's joy.

When the celebrant had finished her words, Cecilia smiled and saw her love reflected back in Linc's eyes, and she said, with all the conviction in her heart, 'I do. I *do* take this man to my heart, and I will keep him there forever.'

They kissed, and the strains of the 'Wedding March' rose through the church and filled it.

The party made its procession outside onto the steps, facing a field of spring flowers. Linc and Cecilia, and behind them Brent and Fiona, Alex and Jayne, and then Stacey and a man by the name of Brendan Carroll, who seemed to have some special history with Alex. And, of course, Rosa—the family's wonderful housekeeper, who was so much more.

There were other guests—friends and colleagues from the plant nursery and from elsewhere. The family sent them on to the wedding reception, but instead of staying at the church for hours of wedding photos, they took just a handful in front of the chapel and in that field of spring flowers.

At the end of it, Cecilia glanced about the group. 'I couldn't be happier—and especially to be sharing this day with all of you.' She reached out her hand and clasped her sister's in hers for a long moment. 'I'm so glad you're here, Stacey.'

It wasn't just about the day, and they both knew that. It was about the fact that Stacey had stuck to her word and turned her life around. She'd even managed to be civil about their mother making an excuse for not being there when Cecilia had got her courage together and invited her. It really didn't matter. Cecilia *had* her family, and deep in her heart she knew it.

Linc. Stacey. The others. And...

'Oooh!' Jayne rested her hand over her abdomen and a look of surprise came over her face. She turned to Alex. 'The baby just moved. It was like butterfly wings! That's the first time I've felt it.'

Cecilia's love and happiness expanded even further as she observed the quiet joy shared by the couple.

She saw Fiona glance into Brent's eyes, and they both looked sheepish as they broke into smiles.

Cecilia gave a soft laugh. 'Do you two have something you want to share?'

'We're pregnant, too.' Fiona's smile burst right across her face. 'We weren't going to say anything until after the wedding.'

At this, it wasn't Cecilia who laughed but Linc, who unexpectedly threw his head back. But he quickly sobered and clasped Cecilia's hand, and all his hope and love were in his eyes, too.

'We were waiting for Stacey to be here for the wedding…' he began.

'To tell you all that we also may have pre-empted the baby part,' Cecilia finished for him.

'Oh, my God!'

'That's wonderful!'

'That's the best news!'

'I'm going to be an uncle once more than I thought.'

Everyone broke into happy speech at once, and then Stacey spoke quietly into the midst of it.

'I will guarantee you're having twins.'

She said it with such conviction that Cecilia's eyes widened.

'So it's just as well I'm around now, because you're going to need me once they come along.'

Brendan Carroll, the man at Stacey's side, gave a low laugh. 'Double the trouble? I like the sound of that.'

Stacey looked startled and a little intrigued. 'Are you planning to be in Sydney for a while?'

'Actually, I just opened a gallery in the city.'

Cecilia looked at her sister's glowing face, at all

the happiness around her, and suspected that Stacey was going to be just fine.

And her sister was probably right about the possibility of twins, too. Cecilia had a feeling about that herself.

Whether one baby or two, Cecilia would indeed want her sister to be a big part of her life from now on.

'Shall we go to this reception?' Linc whispered the words into her ear. 'The sooner we arrive, the sooner I can sneak you away so I can have you to myself. I want to discuss the possibility of twins…' Love and warmth and desire mingled in his gaze. 'Among other things.'

And so Mr and Mrs Linc MacKay led the family—*their family*—towards the cars that would take them to the reception.

As Linc settled beside Cecilia in the back seat of their chauffer-driven car, he couldn't believe how happy she had made him and went on making him in every single moment.

'I can't imagine life without you now, and I'm longing for this child or these children to join us. Do you think your sister is right?'

Cecilia's contentment flooded over, and she blinked to dispel the sudden rise of emotional tears to her eyes.

She glanced down. 'It would explain why I've had to have this dress let out three times in the last month, even though I'm so early along in the pregnancy.'

Linc gave a delighted laugh. 'Cecilia MacKay, I love you with all my heart and I always will. Did you know that?'

And, actually, Cecilia did!

* * * * *

MILLS & BOON®
Hardback – April 2016

ROMANCE

The Sicilian's Stolen Son	Lynne Graham
Seduced into Her Boss's Service	Cathy Williams
The Billionaire's Defiant Acquisition	Sharon Kendrick
One Night to Wedding Vows	Kim Lawrence
Engaged to Her Ravensdale Enemy	Melanie Milburne
A Diamond Deal with the Greek	Maya Blake
Inherited by Ferranti	Kate Hewitt
The Secret to Marrying Marchesi	Amanda Cinelli
The Billionaire's Baby Swap	Rebecca Winters
The Wedding Planner's Big Day	Cara Colter
Holiday with the Best Man	Kate Hardy
Tempted by Her Tycoon Boss	Jennie Adams
Seduced by the Heart Surgeon	Carol Marinelli
Falling for the Single Dad	Emily Forbes
The Fling That Changed Everything	Alison Roberts
A Child to Open Their Hearts	Marion Lennox
The Greek Doctor's Secret Son	Jennifer Taylor
Caught in a Storm of Passion	Lucy Ryder
Take Me, Cowboy	Maisey Yates
His Baby Agenda	Katherine Garbera

MILLS & BOON®
Large Print – April 2016

ROMANCE

The Price of His Redemption	Carol Marinelli
Back in the Brazilian's Bed	Susan Stephens
The Innocent's Sinful Craving	Sara Craven
Brunetti's Secret Son	Maya Blake
Talos Claims His Virgin	Michelle Smart
Destined for the Desert King	Kate Walker
Ravensdale's Defiant Captive	Melanie Milburne
The Best Man & The Wedding Planner	Teresa Carpenter
Proposal at the Winter Ball	Jessica Gilmore
Bodyguard...to Bridegroom?	Nikki Logan
Christmas Kisses with Her Boss	Nina Milne

HISTORICAL

His Christmas Countess	Louise Allen
The Captain's Christmas Bride	Annie Burrows
Lord Lansbury's Christmas Wedding	Helen Dickson
Warrior of Fire	Michelle Willingham
Lady Rowena's Ruin	Carol Townend

MEDICAL

The Baby of Their Dreams	Carol Marinelli
Falling for Her Reluctant Sheikh	Amalie Berlin
Hot-Shot Doc, Secret Dad	Lynne Marshall
Father for Her Newborn Baby	Lynne Marshall
His Little Christmas Miracle	Emily Forbes
Safe in the Surgeon's Arms	Molly Evans

MILLS & BOON®
Hardback – May 2016

ROMANCE

Morelli's Mistress	Anne Mather
A Tycoon to Be Reckoned With	Julia James
Billionaire Without a Past	Carol Marinelli
The Shock Cassano Baby	Andie Brock
The Most Scandalous Ravensdale	Melanie Milburne
The Sheikh's Last Mistress	Rachael Thomas
Claiming the Royal Innocent	Jennifer Hayward
Kept at the Argentine's Command	Lucy Ellis
The Billionaire Who Saw Her Beauty	Rebecca Winters
In the Boss's Castle	Jessica Gilmore
One Week with the French Tycoon	Christy McKellen
Rafael's Contract Bride	Nina Milne
Tempted by Hollywood's Top Doc	Louisa George
Perfect Rivals...	Amy Ruttan
English Rose in the Outback	Lucy Clark
A Family for Chloe	Lucy Clark
The Doctor's Baby Secret	Scarlet Wilson
Married for the Boss's Baby	Susan Carlisle
Twins for the Texan	Charlene Sands
Secret Baby Scandal	Joanne Rock

MILLS & BOON®
Large Print – May 2016

ROMANCE

The Queen's New Year Secret	Maisey Yates
Wearing the De Angelis Ring	Cathy Williams
The Cost of the Forbidden	Carol Marinelli
Mistress of His Revenge	Chantelle Shaw
Theseus Discovers His Heir	Michelle Smart
The Marriage He Must Keep	Dani Collins
Awakening the Ravensdale Heiress	Melanie Milburne
His Princess of Convenience	Rebecca Winters
Holiday with the Millionaire	Scarlet Wilson
The Husband She'd Never Met	Barbara Hannay
Unlocking Her Boss's Heart	Christy McKellen

HISTORICAL

In Debt to the Earl	Elizabeth Rolls
Rake Most Likely to Seduce	Bronwyn Scott
The Captain and His Innocent	Lucy Ashford
Scoundrel of Dunborough	Margaret Moore
One Night with the Viking	Harper St. George

MEDICAL

A Touch of Christmas Magic	Scarlet Wilson
Her Christmas Baby Bump	Robin Gianna
Winter Wedding in Vegas	Janice Lynn
One Night Before Christmas	Susan Carlisle
A December to Remember	Sue MacKay
A Father This Christmas?	Louisa Heaton